# HELLO, UNIVERSE

# ERIN ENTRADA KELLY

HELLO, UNIVERSE

Greenwillow Books
*An Imprint of* HarperCollins*Publishers*

Hello, Universe
Text copyright © 2017 by Erin Entrada Kelly;
illustrations copyright © 2017 by Isabel Roxas

The text of this book is set in ITC Usherwood
Book design by Sylvie Le Floc'h

Library of Congress Cataloging-in-Publication Data
Names: Kelly, Erin Entrada, author.
Title: Hello universe / Erin Entrada Kelly.
Description: First edition. | New York, NY: Greenwillow Books, an imprint of HarperCollins Publishers, [2017] | Summary: Lives of four misfits are intertwined when a bully's prank lands shy Virgil at the bottom of a well and Valencia, Kaori, and Gen band together in an epic quest to find and rescue him.
Identifiers: LCCN 2016022723 | ISBN 9780062414151 (hardback)
Subjects: | CYAC: Friendship—Fiction. | Missing children—Fiction. | Bullying—Fiction. | Hearing impaired—Fiction. | Psychic ability—Fiction. | Sisters—Fiction. | BISAC: JUVENILE FICTION / Social Issues / Friendship. | JUVENILE FICTION / Social Issues / Self-Esteem & Self-Reliance. | JUVENILE FICTION / Social Issues / Special Needs.
Classification: LCC PZ7.1.K45 Hel 2017 | DDC [Fic]—dc23 LC record available at https://lccn.loc.gov/2016022723

18 19 20 21 22 CG/LSCH 10 9
First Edition

Greenwillow Books

To Carolanne, my beautifully complex Aquarius

And Jen Breen—Gemini, phoenix, visionary

# 1
## Grand Failure

Eleven-year-old Virgil Salinas already regretted the rest of middle school, and he'd only just finished sixth grade. He imagined all those years stretching ahead of him like a long line of hurdles, each of them getting taller, thicker, and heavier, and him standing in front of them on his weak and skinny legs. He was no good at hurdles. He'd found this out the hard way: in gym class, where he was the smallest, most forgettable, and always picked last.

All things considered, he should have been happy on the last day of school. The year was over. He should have been skipping home, ready to tackle the bright summer ahead. Instead he walked through the front door like a defeated athlete—head low, shoulders hunched, a sack of disappointment sitting on his chest like an anvil. Because today, it was official: he was a Grand Failure.

"Oy, Virgilio," said his grandmother—his Lola— when he came in. She didn't look up. She was in the kitchen, slicing a mango. "Come take one of these. Your mother bought too many again. They were on sale, so she buys ten. And what do we need ten mangoes for? They're not even from the Philippines. They're from Venezuela. Your mother bought ten Venezuelan mangoes, and for what? That woman would buy kisses from Judas if they were on sale."

She shook her head.

Virgil straightened his posture so Lola wouldn't

suspect anything was wrong. He took a mango from the fruit bowl. Lola's eyebrows immediately scrunched together. Only they weren't really eyebrows, because she'd plucked them clean.

"What's wrong? Why you have that look?" she said.

"What look?" Virgil said.

"You know." Lola didn't like to explain herself. "Is that pug-faced boy at school being mean to you again?"

"No, Lola." For once, that was the least of his worries. "Everything's fine."

"Hmm," said Lola. She knew everything wasn't fine. She noticed everything about him. They had a secret kinship. It'd been that way ever since the first day she'd come from the Philippines to live with them. On the morning she arrived, Virgil's parents and identical twin brothers immediately rushed her in a flood of hugs and hellos. With the exception of Virgil, that's how the Salinas family was—big personalities that bubbled over like pots of soup. Virgil felt like unbuttered toast standing next to them.

"*Ay sus*, my first moments in America will be filled with a pulsing headache," Lola said. She pressed her fingertips to her temples and waved toward Virgil's older brothers, who were tall and lean and muscled, even then. "Joselito, Julius, fetch my bags, hah? I want to say hello to my youngest grandson."

After Joselito and Julius scurried off—ever the helpful brothers—Virgil's parents presented him like a rare exhibit they didn't quite understand.

"This is Turtle," his mother said.

That was their name for him: Turtle. Because he wouldn't "come out of his shell." Every time they said it, a piece of him broke.

Lola had squatted in front of him and whispered, "You are my favorite, Virgilio." Then she put her fingers to her lips and said, "Don't tell your brothers."

That was six years ago, and he knew he was still her favorite, even though she'd never said so again.

He could trust Lola. And maybe one day he would confess his secret to her, the one that made him a Grand Failure. But not now. Not today.

Lola took the mango from him.

"Let me slice that for you," she said.

Virgil stood next to her and watched. Lola was old and her fingers felt like paper, but she sliced mangoes like an artist. She started slowly, biding her time. "You know," she began, "I had a dream about the Stone Boy again last night."

She'd been dreaming about the Stone Boy for days now. The dream was always the same: a shy boy—not unlike Virgil—gets terribly lonely, takes a walk in the forest, and begs a rock to eat him. The biggest stone opens its gravelly mouth and the boy jumps inside, never to be seen again. When his parents find the stone, there is nothing they can do. Virgil wasn't sure how hard his parents would try to get him out anyway, but he knew Lola would hand chisel that rock to pieces if she had to.

"I promise not to jump into any rocks," Virgil said.

"I know there's something going on with you, *anak*. You have the face of Frederico the Sorrowful."

"Who is Frederico the Sorrowful?"

"He was a boy king who was sad all the time. But he didn't want anyone to know he was sad, because he wanted people to think he was a strong king. But one day he couldn't hold in his sorrows anymore. It all came out, just like a fountain." She lifted her hands in the air to mimic splashing water, still holding the paring knife in one of them. "He wept and wept until the whole land flooded and all the islands drifted away from each other. He wound up trapped on an island all alone until a crocodile came and ate him." She handed a beautiful slice of mango to Virgil. "Here."

Virgil took it. "Lola, can I ask you a question?"

"If you ever have a question, ask it."

"How come so many of your stories have boys getting eaten by stuff, like rocks or crocodiles?"

"Not all of them are about boys getting eaten. Sometimes it's girls." Lola tossed the knife into the sink and raised her non-eyebrows. "If you decide to talk, you come find your Lola. Don't burst like a fountain and float away."

"Okay," Virgil said. "I'm going to my room to check on Gulliver, make sure he's okay."

Gulliver, his pet guinea pig, was always happy to see him. He would chirp as soon as Virgil opened the door; he knew it. Maybe he wouldn't feel like such a failure then.

"Why wouldn't he be okay?" Lola called out as Virgil walked toward his room. "Guinea pigs can't get in much trouble, *anak*."

Virgil could hear her laughing as he placed the mango between his teeth.

# 2
## Valencia

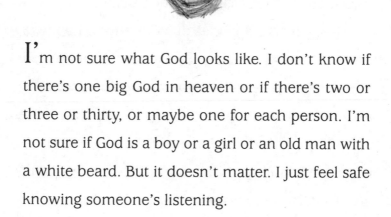

I'm not sure what God looks like. I don't know if there's one big God in heaven or if there's two or three or thirty, or maybe one for each person. I'm not sure if God is a boy or a girl or an old man with a white beard. But it doesn't matter. I just feel safe knowing someone's listening.

I mostly talk to Saint Rene. His real name is Renatus Goupil. He was a French missionary who traveled to Canada. While he was there, he made the sign of the cross over a kid's head and they thought he was spreading curses, so they took him prisoner and killed him.

I found out about him because on my tenth birthday, this girl Roberta gave me a book called *Famous Deaf People in History*. I would have never given Roberta a book about *Famous Blond People* or *Famous People Who Talk Too Much* or *Famous People Who Tried to Cheat Off My Spelling Paper*—all of which describe Roberta—but the good thing was that I found out about Saint Rene.

I don't know sign language but I taught myself the alphabet so I made up a sign name for Saint Rene. I cross my middle finger over my index finger—the sign for R—and tap it three times lightly against my lips. That's one of the first things I do after I take off my hearing aids for the night. Then I stare at the ceiling and imagine my prayers traveling up, up, up and hovering over my bed until they lift all the way through the roof. Then I imagine them landing on a cloud and sitting there, waiting to be answered.

When I was younger, I thought the cloud would get so heavy that all my prayers would come falling down and I'd have everything I wished for, but now I'm eleven so I know better. I still picture them sailing up, though. There's no harm in that.

I only pray at night, because it's my least favorite time of day. Everything is still and dark, and I have too much time to think. One thought leads to another until it's two in the morning and I haven't slept a wink. Or I've slept, but not well.

I didn't always hate the nighttime.

I used to crawl into bed and drift off to sleep, no problem.

It's not because of the dark. That's never bothered me. One time my parents took me to this place called Crystal Caverns where you went underground and couldn't even see your hand in front of your face. I wasn't scared at all. I loved it down there. I felt like an explorer. Afterward my dad bought me a souvenir snow globe, only there are bats inside instead of snow. I keep it right next to me, on my nightstand, and I shake it before I go to sleep, just because.

So it's not the dark that keeps me awake.

It's the nightmare.

The nightmare goes like this.

I'm standing in a big open field—one I've never stood in before. The grass is yellow and brown under my feet, and I'm surrounded by thick crowds of people. Nightmare Me knows who they are, even though they don't look like anyone I know in real life. They all look at me with round black eyes. Eyes without whites in them. Then a girl in a blue dress steps forward, away from the crowd. She says two words: "solar eclipse." I know what she's saying even though I'm not wearing my hearing aids and she doesn't move her mouth. That's how it is in dreams sometimes.

The girl is pointing skyward.

Nightmare Me looks up to where she's pointing and watches attentively, not scared yet. I crane my neck, along with everyone else. We all watch as the moon moves in front of the sun. The blazing blue sky turns gray, then dark, and Nightmare Me thinks it's the most amazing thing I've ever seen.

It's strange how nightmares work, though.

Somehow Nightmare Me knows things won't end well. As soon as the moon finishes passing the sun, my blood rushes into my ears and my palms dampen with sweat. I look down from the sky—slowly, slowly, not wanting to see—and just as I suspected, everyone is gone. The whole crowd. Even the girl in the dress. Nothing moves. Not one single blade of grass. The field stretches on for miles and miles. The moon has pulled everyone away. All but Nightmare Me.

I'm the only person on the face of the earth.

∗∗∗

I can't tell what time it is, but I know it's late. Like, past-midnight late. As hard as I want to not think about the nightmare, here I am, lying in bed and thinking about it. I shake my Crystal Caverns globe and watch the bats flutter around. Then I try to focus on the bumpy paint on my bedroom ceiling. My dad calls it popcorn paint. When I was a little girl, we'd pretend the ceiling was really made of popcorn and we'd open our mouths wide, wide and let it fall in.

"Next time I'll paint a licorice ceiling," my dad would say. He liked to say that Twizzlers were one of his favorite food groups. I'd shake my head and say, "Chocolate, chocolate, chocolate."

It was our routine. But we don't do things like that anymore.

I don't think he knows how to be a dad to an eleven-year-old girl. You can't sit an eleven-year-old girl on your shoulders, especially not when she's all knees and elbows and five foot five, and you can't make hot chocolate and wait up for Santa Claus or read picture books.

But it was still nice to remember the popcorn-licorice-chocolate ceiling.

It's better than thinking about the nightmare.

I close my eyes and feel the hum of the ceiling fan against my cheeks. I make a promise to myself: if I have another nightmare tonight, I'll talk to someone and ask for help. I don't know who. But someone. Not my mom.

Don't get me wrong. There are times when my mom is easy to talk to. If you catch her on a good day, she isn't too mom-like. But I can never tell which mom I'll get. Sometimes she is overprotective, overbearing, overeverything. I once asked her flat out if she treated me that way because I'm deaf, because that's what it feels like sometimes.

"I'm not overprotective because you're deaf. I'm overprotective because I'm your mother," she'd said.

But something in her eyes told me that wasn't the whole truth and nothing but the truth.

I'm good at reading eyes. Same as lips.

I most definitely don't want Mom to know about the nightmare. She'd start asking me about it every morning and every night and insist that I see a psychiatrist or something.

Then again, maybe that wouldn't be so bad.

Maybe then I'd get some sleep.

I close my eyes.

*Think of something nice.*

The coming summer. Yes. That's what I'll think about. Sixth grade is over and the nice, lazy summer stretches ahead. Okay, so maybe I don't have a gazillion friends to hang out with. So what? I'll make my own fun. I'll explore the woods and take notes for my zoological diary. Maybe draw some bird sketches.

There is plenty to do.

I don't need a gazillion friends.

I don't even need one.

All I need is me, right?

Solo—it's the best way to go.

It's a lot less trouble.

# 3
# Help of a Different Nature

Gulliver was a good friend, guinea pig or not. Virgil could tell him anything and he wouldn't judge. And that's what Virgil needed, only he also needed real, practical guidance.

He needed help of a different nature.

Lola had once told Virgil a story about a woman named Dayapan who'd been hungry for seven years because she didn't know how to grow food. One day Dayapan wept because all she wanted was one grain of rice and one pea pod—anything to put in her belly. She took a bath in a spring to wash away her tears, and a Great Spirit appeared to her with armfuls of sugarcane and rice. The Great Spirit gave it all to Dayapan and told her exactly what she needed to do to grow more. Dayapan was never hungry again.

Virgil wished that he had a Great Spirit that could tell him exactly what to do, but he only had Kaori Tanaka.

Virgil fed Gulliver and texted Kaori as he walked down the hall for breakfast. Under normal circumstances, he wouldn't text someone at seven forty-five in the morning, especially not on the first day of summer—but nothing about Kaori was normal. Besides, she always seemed to be awake.

> need appointment this
> afternoon if thats ok

Virgil slipped his phone into the pocket of his pajamas and followed the unmistakable sounds of his parents and brothers, who were early risers because they seemed to have an endless stream of soccer practices.

In the kitchen, Mom, Dad, and the J's were drinking orange juice and letting their personalities bubble over, while Virgil tried to maneuver through all the excitement so he could get a piece of fruit or boil an egg.

"Good morning, Virgilio!" said Joselito.

"Good morning, Turtle," said his parents, almost in unison.

Then Julius: "*Maayong buntag*, little brother."

Virgil grumbled something like hello. His parents and brothers were sitting in the high-back chairs at the counter. Lola was at the breakfast table, reading the newspaper.

"Your mother bought too many clementines, so eat as many as you can," said Lola without looking up. Then she clucked her tongue at all the wastefulness. Virgil grabbed two clementines in each hand and tried hard not to drop them as he sat next to her. His phone buzzed in his pocket.

"What're you reading about, Lola?" Virgil asked. He arranged the clementines in a perfect line in front of him, then checked his phone.

> I am available. Be here at noon SHARP!

Virgil laid the phone facedown on the table next to the clementines.

"Death and destruction across the universe," said Lola. "Godlessness around every corner."

Julius craned his neck their way. "Aw, Lola, don't be such a downer."

Virgil had long suspected that his brothers were crafted out of a factory that made perfect, athletic, perpetually happy children, and he was made from all the leftover parts. The only sign that something went wrong with Joselito and Julius were their pinkie fingers, which turned slightly inward.

Virgil studied his own hands as they worked away at the peel on a clementine. His fingers were long and slender. None of them turned inward.

"Lola, do you know anything about hands?" he asked. He glanced at Joselito and Julius, but they were busy talking about soccer. Their father had recently joined a grown-up soccer league. Everyone was wild about soccer except Virgil.

Lola set down her newspaper. "I know that they have five fingers each, most of the time."

"What do you mean, most of the time?"

"I once knew a girl in my village who was born with an extra thumb."

"Really? What did they do with it? Did she go to the doctor and get it chopped off?"

"No. Her family was poor. They couldn't afford a doctor."

"What did they do, then?"

"Kept the extra thumb. What else?"

"Did she feel like a freak?"

"Maybe. But I told her God must know something she didn't, and that's why He did it."

"Maybe He wanted her to be an excellent hitchhiker," Virgil said.

"Maybe. Or maybe she was like Ruby San Salvador."

"Who is Ruby San Salvador?"

"Another girl from my village. She had seven sisters. Each time one of them was born, her parents had their fortunes read. But when they got to Ruby San Salvador, no one was able to see her future. Any time someone tried, they just got a blank picture. No one knew what it meant. She walked around all the time saying, 'What is my destiny? What is my destiny?' Finally I said, 'No one knows, but you're driving us all crazy.'"

Virgil thought of poor Ruby San Salvador,

watching all her sisters get something that she couldn't have.

"What happened to her?" Virgil asked.

"She left to go figure it out. The village got much quieter without all the questions." Lola narrowed her eyes at him. "What's this about, Virgilio? Of all the questions in the world you could ask, why are you asking about hands?"

"I just noticed that all my fingers are nice and straight. Don't you think?"

He set the clementine peels aside and put his hands on the table to show her.

Lola nodded. "Yes, you have beautiful hands. You have the hands of a gifted pianist. We should put you in piano lessons. Li!" she called to Virgil's mother. "Li!"

"Yes, *manang*?" said Virgil's mother, who was in the middle of laughing. She was always in the middle of laughing.

"How come we never put Virgilio in piano

lessons, hah? He has the hands of a pianist!"

But Virgil's father answered instead. "Because boys need to play sports, not fool around on a silly piano. Right, Turtle?"

Virgil shoved half a clementine in his mouth.

Mr. Salinas lifted his glass of orange juice. "He just needs to put meat on his bones!"

Lola fixed her eyes on Virgil's hands and shook her head. *"Ay sus,"* she mumbled. "You should play the piano, *anak*. You could play in Madison Square Garden with fingers like that. I have no doubt!"

"Maybe I'll take lessons," Virgil said, his voice garbled from the fruit.

"Yes, yes, good idea, good idea," said Lola. She shifted her eyes to his face and studied it. "You feeling better today, *anak*?"

Virgil swallowed the clementine and nodded.

"Hmm," said Lola. "How is that little pet of yours?"

"He's okay. But last night I read online that

guinea pigs aren't supposed to live alone because they're very social animals."

"So?"

"So, Gulliver's alone."

"Is that what's bothering you?"

Gulliver had nothing to do with his Grand Failure. And normally Virgil wouldn't tell a lie. But this was a situation where saying yes would kill two birds with one stone (or feed two birds with one seed, as Kaori liked to say). He might get another guinea pig, and Lola would stop asking about his sorrowful face.

So he said, "Yes?"

Lola nodded. She didn't understand why anyone would want a pet guinea pig, but everyone knew what it was like to be lonely.

"I'll talk to your mother," she said.

# 4
## Bells of the Buddhist Monastery

Twelve-year-old Kaori Tanaka—a proud Gemini—liked to tell people her parents were born in the high, misty mountains of a samurai village. In truth, they were both second-generation Japanese-Americans from Ohio. No matter. Kaori knew in her bones that they were meant to be born in the mountains. Sometimes people were just delivered to the wrong birthplace. How else could she explain her powers of second sight, which could only come from someplace magical?

Kaori was mildly surprised to get a text from one of her clients (her only client, truth be told) on the first day of summer, particularly at seven forty-five in the morning. But the night before, just as she was gliding to sleep, she'd had the vision of a hawk perched on a giant fence post. Only now she realized it must have been a vulture, not a hawk. And vulture started with *V*, just like Virgil's name. The connection couldn't have been clearer.

She was already awake—she believed in waking up with the dawn whenever possible—when she heard the bells of a Buddhist monastery chime from her phone. A text message alert. She snatched it immediately and read Virgil's message.

"This must be a matter of some urgency," she said, from her bed. She liked to talk aloud when she was alone, just in case any spirits were listening.

After replying to the text, Kaori lit a stick of incense, walked across her zodiac circle rug, and stepped into the hallway. She knocked gently on her younger sister's bedroom door. No one was awake yet, least of all seven-year-old Gen. Gen was a Cancer; morning wasn't her best time of day. Cancers were notorious night owls.

"Knocking is fruitless," Kaori said.

She opened the door and was once again assaulted and mildly offended by her sister's hot-pink dresser, hot-pink curtains, hot-pink rug, and hot-pink comforter. It was truly the room of a second grader, complete with teddy bears scattered all over the floor and plastic teacups and teapots toppled here and there. Gen was monstrously untidy. She also had a tendency to run through hobbies. Gen was determined to become the champion of something one day. It used to be hopscotch. Then monkey bars. Then checkers. There was a discarded recorder on the floor that she had once planned to master and a chapter book on Abraham Lincoln from the time she decided to become an amateur historian. A pink jump rope lay coiled like a snake near the foot of the narrow twin bed—evidence of her latest obsession.

"One day she'll mature," Kaori said, to the spirits. She walked up to her sister and kicked the jump rope out of the way with a sigh of irritation. Gen had been jump roping around the house for a week straight, driving everyone mad. She'd already broken three water glasses.

"Gen," Kaori said, poking her sister's shoulder. "Wake up. We have a client coming today, and we need to prepare."

Gen's eyelids fluttered but didn't open.

"Gen." Kaori poked a little harder. Her sister was wearing bunny-print pajamas. Really. "Get up."

Gen grumbled and pulled the comforter over her head.

Kaori smoothed the front of her own pajamas—coal black, with red trim—and said, "Okay, then. I'll just prepare the spirit stones alone."

Gen tossed off the covers, eyes wide. Her dark hair stuck up in every direction. "You're using the spirit stones?"

"I have reason to suspect I'll need them. Just a sense. But if you're too busy sleeping . . ."

"I'm getting up, I'm getting up." And she did.

"Meet me in the spirit chamber," Kaori said. She waved toward Gen's pajamas. "But get rid of the bunnies first."

# 5
## Turtle

It was true about guinea pigs. They weren't supposed to live alone. Virgil wished he'd never learned that, because now he was convinced that Gulliver suffered from debilitating depression. The poor black-and-white rodent had been by himself for the past eighteen months, and Virgil couldn't help but think he'd been pining the hours away in desperate loneliness.

Before his appointment with Kaori, Virgil

unloaded everything from his backpack and stuffed it with fleece blankets that he secretly swiped from the linen closet. Then he tucked Gulliver inside. They would journey together to the Tanakas. Then neither of them would have to be alone.

Gulliver didn't chirp once when Virgil lifted him out of his cage—another sign of his misery and resentment.

"The guy at the pet shop didn't tell me guinea pigs were social creatures," Virgil said, staring into Gulliver's beady, round black eyes. "I'm sorry."

Virgil set Gulliver carefully atop the blankets and zipped the backpack. He made sure to leave it partially open so Gulliver could breathe.

"If it makes you feel any better, I know what you're going through," he said. At the moment, Virgil's Grand Failure made them kindred spirits.

Once Gulliver was tucked safely away, Virgil pulled the straps over his shoulders. It was a Thursday, which meant his mother didn't work at the hospital until the night shift. She was on the couch with her legs tucked up, watching something on television. This was a disappointment, since Virgil hoped to slip out the front door without having an actual conversation with either of his parents.

No such luck.

"Where you going, Turtle?" she asked.

When they called him Turtle, it was like when Chet Bullens at school called him a retard. He knew his parents weren't like Chet Bullens, but he also knew that they were poking fun at his shyness, just like Chet Bullens was making fun of the fact that Virgil was eleven years old and didn't know his multiplication tables.

Did they know how much he hated that nickname?

"Kaori's," Virgil mumbled.

Mrs. Salinas and Mrs. Tanaka knew each other from the hospital. They were both nurses.

"Bring her a mango and tell her not to eat it until it's ripe."

Virgil hurried to the kitchen, conscious of the passing minutes, and snatched a mango from the fruit bowl. Lola had been complaining about his mother's fruit buying for the past three days, so he knew his mom was trying to prove a point by putting every mango and clementine to good use.

Just as he turned the knob of the front door, his mother said, "Don't wander too far, Turtle. *Mahal kita.* Be careful."

He hesitated at the half-open door. "Mom?"

"Yeah?"

*Don't call me that.*

*It makes me feel like I'm six years old.*

*It makes me feel like a loser.*

*"Mahal kita,"* he said, which meant "I love you."

He stepped into the warm sun.

# 6
# The Tiger of Elm Street

The Tanakas lived in an ordinary house on the opposite side of dense, hilly woods, at 1401 Maple Street. It wasn't a far walk for Virgil; just cut through the woods, cross Elm and Ash, and voilà, he was there. But that would've just been too easy. Instead, fate (or bad luck, Virgil wasn't sure which) had placed Chet Bullens's house directly on the way to the Tanakas', at 1417 Elm. And ninety percent of the time Chet, aka the Bull, was in his driveway shooting a basketball. Virgil's parents complained that kids today never spent any time outside because they were too busy playing video games. But not the Bull. He haunted Elm Street like a tiger on the loose.

Virgil didn't think of him as the Bull just because Chet's last name was Bullens. The kid really was like a bull. Always ready to charge, always fired up to call Virgil a retard or pansy. Sometimes Virgil expected smoke to come spewing from Chet Bullens's nostrils.

Virgil had to go several blocks out of his way to avoid 1417 Elm. It added minutes to the trip, but what else could he do? So when he emerged from the woods facing Elm Street, he immediately veered left, even though he could've walked one block right, crossed the street, and been at the Tanakas' in no time at all.

He kept his head down and hooked his thumbs through the straps of his backpack. *Walk, walk, walk. When you reach the house on*

*the corner with the green door, turn right.*

For whatever reason, Virgil had it in his head that if he didn't make eye contact with anything, he would go unnoticed.

Not so.

"Hey, retard!"

It came from behind him, a fairly good distance. But that didn't mean anything. The Bull knew how to close distances faster than a speeding bullet.

Virgil's heart gave one super-loud *THUMP*.

The turn-at-the-green-door plan wasn't a fail-safe. Sometimes Chet wandered away from his house, thick hands still holding his basketball. It was inevitable.

Virgil didn't look up. He picked up his pace.

"Hey, RETARD! Don't you know your own name?"

Virgil's back dripped with sweat as he walked even faster. The sun was either getting hotter or Virgil's nerves were getting weaker.

He heard quick movement behind him. Sneakers on concrete.

Would the Bull push him down from behind?
Bounce the basketball off his head? At school he
usually just shoved him into the wall. The Bull had
never actually thrown him down or beaten him up
or anything. But there was a first time for everything.

The Bull's sneakers came into view. Virgil
smelled the Bull's sweat and wondered if that's
how he smelled too.

"Where you goin', retardo?" the Bull asked,
walking alongside him like they were old buddies.

Virgil didn't answer. *Walk, walk, walk.*

"Hey, lemme ask you something," the Bull
continued. "What's five times five?"

*Walk, walk, walk.*

"You're a retardo, so you probably don't know,
but five times five equals the number of times I
made out with your sister."

The Bull howled with laughter. *Walk, walk.*
Virgil imagined an alternate reality, one where he
stopped—feet firmly planted on the ground—and

looked Chet Bullens square in the eye.

"I don't even have a sister, ignoramus," Alternate Virgil would say. Then he'd grab the Bull's shirt collar in his skinny little hand, the one with the fingers of a gifted pianist, and shove him against the nearest tree. "Take it back," he'd say. But the Bull wouldn't be able to talk because his collar would be too tight, so Virgil would lift him up with one hand and throw him across the neighborhood. The Bull would fly over thirty rooftops before landing on top of someone's chimney, which would be burning hot even though it was summer and no one was using their fireplace. And he'd get stuck there and start cooking like a lump of pot roast.

But Alternate Virgil didn't exist. Only Turtle. So instead of saying a single word, Virgil took off running.

The Bull didn't chase him. He just laughed and laughed.

# 7

## A Peculiar Future

Even after the Bull was out of sight, the laughter followed Virgil like a buzzing housefly until he finally reached the plain redbrick home of the Tanakas.

It was hard to believe that someone like Kaori lived in such an ordinary house. Then again, her parents were the ones who had bought it, and Virgil knew from firsthand experience that kids can't pick their parents.

Gen opened the front door, just a smidge.

A pink jump rope looped behind her neck like a stethoscope. Virgil remembered the last time he'd jumped rope in gym class. It hadn't gone well.

"Password?" she said.

"I've been here five times. Do I have to—"

*"Password."*

Virgil sighed. "Venus rises in the west."

Gen nodded and stepped aside. Virgil glanced down at the clock on his phone. He was right on time, despite everything. He already smelled the incense drifting down the hall from Kaori's room, which she called "the spirit chamber." Her room was spare. Other than her bed and rug, there was a table for incense, an enormous, complicated poster of constellations tacked to one of the walls, and books shoved in corners.

Kaori sat cross-legged on the rug with a small drawstring bag in her lap. Incense smoke curled over her head and disappeared. Gen sat down next to her. Virgil sat down and perched his backpack carefully on his lap. Then he set the mango on the rug in front of him.

"My mom told me to bring you this. But don't eat it until it's ripe," he said.

Kaori nodded at Gen, who picked up the mango with both hands and set it aside.

Virgil peeked inside his backpack to check on Gulliver.

"Would you like Gen to take your things?" Kaori asked.

"No," Virgil replied quickly. "My guinea pig's in here."

Gen's eyes lit up. "Really?" She made a move toward the bag, but Kaori told her to sit down.

"You have a *rodent* in your backpack?" said Kaori, narrowing her darkly lined eyes.

"Technically, yes," said Virgil. "But it's not like it's a rat or anything. It's a guinea pig."

"Rodents are rodents." Kaori paused. "Now. Let's get down to business."

She lifted the drawstring bag. It looked like a sack of marbles, but when Virgil reached inside, he realized they were medium-sized stones, like the kind his mother used in the garden.

"Just pick one. Don't look. Then put it on the rug between us," Kaori said.

The rock he selected was nothing special, as far as he could tell. Gray, smooth, kind of shaped like a crescent moon.

Kaori studied it like an archaeologist. Then she sat up straight and closed her eyes.

"You have a very peculiar future ahead of you," she said. She placed her index fingers to her temples. Her dark hair was brushed out and spiked up, like she'd just stuck her finger in an electrical socket, and her lips were painted a light shade of blue. "Mm-hmm. Very peculiar."

"In what way?" asked Virgil.

Kaori pressed her lips together.

"Shh."

Gulliver sneezed.

"Something will happen to you," Kaori continued.

Virgil looked at Gen. She shrugged.

"That's it?" said Virgil. "Something will happen to me?"

"I see darkness," said Kaori.

"Your eyes are closed."

She sighed without opening her eyes. "I know my eyes are closed, dummy. That's not what I meant."

"What did you mean, then?"

"What I mean is, I see you in a dark place."

"Dark how?"

"Just dark."

Virgil's heart pounded. Tha-*THUMP*.

His second most confidential piece of information: he was afraid of the dark. Yes, he was eleven and shouldn't be afraid anymore, but he couldn't help it. Maybe it was the tales Lola told him about evil three-headed monkeys that thrived in the

 44

darkness, or her stories of bad children who were plucked up by birds in the dead of night. Darkness was a sightless beast, as far as Virgil was concerned.

He swallowed a lump the size of Chet's basketball.

"I don't see anything else," Kaori said. She opened her eyes, then reached across Gen to pick up the mango. She sniffed it. "How will I know when this is ripe?"

"It'll be soft, but not too soft," said Virgil. He pushed his fear to the corner of his brain and checked on Gulliver again. "Listen, I actually came here because I have a specific problem."

"What kind of problem?"

He looked at Kaori, then Gen, and pulled all his thoughts together. He imagined the words standing up in a perfect line and coming out of his mouth clearly, without stuttering or skipping or sounding stupid. This was a big deal. He was about to reveal his first most confidential piece of top-secret information. The one that made him a Grand Failure.

"Uh . . . ," he said.

Kaori tossed the mango from hand to hand.

"The thing is . . . ," he continued, ". . . there's this girl that I know—well, I mean, that I want to talk to, and uh—well, I've been kinda planning to talk to her since the beginning of the school year, but uh . . . the year is over now . . . and well, um . . . I never exactly introduced myself. But I, uh, kinda have this feeling that we were meant to be friends, you know, like—"

"Like a premonition!" said Kaori. She set the mango down on the rug, on the sign for Aquarius.

"Yeah, I guess. Sure. Yeah." Virgil's cheeks warmed.

Gen picked at her elbow. "Why didn't you just go up and say, 'Hey, do you wanna be my friend?' That's what I do."

Kaori shot her the evil eye. "Hush, Gen. Virgil and I are in middle school. It doesn't work that way. Besides, Virgil's shy. Can't you see that?"

Flames of humiliation rose from Virgil's chest to his neck.

"I can help you," Kaori said. "What's her name?"

"Uh . . ."

"We don't even go to the same school. You can tell me. I probably don't even know her."

That was true. Kaori went to private school. But still. He wasn't ready to say her name aloud. This whole situation was embarrassing enough.

"Tell me her initials, then," Kaori said.

"Okay." Virgil took a deep breath. "V. S."

Kaori tilted her head, confused. "But those are *your* initials."

"I know."

Kaori's whole demeanor lit up as if she'd just sat on a hot plate. "That's fate! It's like you were meant to be friends! There are no coincidences, Virgil Salinas." Kaori was practically giddy. "Do you know her sign?"

He was almost too humiliated to admit it, but

yes—he knew. All the kids in the Thursday resource room celebrated their birthdays with a sheet cake, and he had made a specific note when it was Valencia's turn.

Birthdays were the only time the whole resource group gathered together. The rest of the time they sat at tables with their one-on-one teacher, working on whatever challenge had put them there. Virgil spent his hour with Ms. Giegrich, learning about numbers, and Valencia spent her time with Mr. King, although Virgil wasn't sure what Valencia needed to learn; she seemed pretty smart. It sounded like all they did was review her homework assignments for the week to make sure she understood everything. Sometimes Mr. King let her spend her hour reading. One time Virgil snuck a look at her book. *Untamed: The Wild Life of Jane Goodall*, it was called. That night he Googled Jane Goodall and found out she was the world's foremost expert on chimpanzees. He promised himself he would read the book too. Someday.

"She's a Scorpio," he said.

"Ooh! Adventurous and courageous! Dynamic yet quick-tempered! Enthusiastic and confident! I can see why you'd be intimidated to talk to V. S. She's so different from you."

Virgil knew she didn't mean that as an insult, but it stung.

Kaori bit her bottom lip, thinking. Gen grabbed the ends of her jump rope and pulled them taut. Virgil looked down at Gulliver.

A few heavy moments of silence ticked by.

"I know just the thing," Kaori said finally. She scooted forward and leaned in like she was about to give Virgil the most valuable piece of knowledge in the history of information. She was so close Virgil could smell her peppermint gum.

"Find five stones, each of a different size. Then bring them to me next Saturday at eleven a.m. sharp. Got it?"

"Got it."

"Oh, and one more thing." Kaori reached into her pocket. "Do you still go with Lola to the Super Saver on Fridays?"

"Yes."

She handed him a business card. "Bring this with you, if you don't mind. Tack it on the bulletin board for me. I would do it myself, but my parents freak out when I give my name and phone number to random strangers."

Virgil took the card from her.

Her cell phone number was printed on the back.

"Put it where people can see," she added.

Virgil said he would.

# 8
# Drama in the Freezer Aisle

"Why are you being so quiet, *anak*?" Lola asked as they turned down the freezer aisle at the Super Saver.

"I'm always quiet," said Virgil.

"Not with your Lola. Besides, I see a different quiet. You have a quiet of the eyes."

"I was just thinking."

"About what?

Virgil paused. "Malaya of the Crocodiles."

It wasn't exactly a lie.

According to Lola, Malaya was a young Filipino girl who once wandered into a starving village. The village was on the bank of a great river where lush fruits and vegetables grew, but no one was allowed to eat anything because it all belonged to the crocodile. One day Malaya appeared. She plucked a guava off the tree and ate it. The villagers were terrified. They told her she couldn't do that or they'd all be killed. But she kept eating. She started a fire and cooked some vegetables. She fed all the villagers. They were scared, but hungry, and they couldn't resist. Sure enough, the crocodile emerged from the water and demanded to know who had eaten all his food. Malaya stepped forward, with the whole village behind her. She jabbed her thumb into her chest—"It was me." The crocodile said he would have to eat the villagers now that they'd taken all his food. When he opened his mouth— sharp teeth glistening—Malaya lifted one of the logs from the fire with her bare hands and shoved it down his throat, killing him.

Malaya wasn't afraid of anything.

Neither was Valencia.

Virgil didn't have to talk to her to know that. He could tell.

"Why Malaya?" Lola asked, snapping him out of the starving village and back into the Super Saver.

He was just about to say it. He was just about to tell her, "I'm thinking of Malaya of the Crocodiles, because there's a girl at school named Valencia who reminds me of her," when the strangest thing happened: Valencia appeared. Right there in the freezer aisle. Valencia Somerset. She was lagging behind her mother and staring blankly at the waffle fries. Neither of them looked very pleased.

It was an odd sensation to be thinking of someone and have her unexpectedly appear. Like thoughts come to life. *It must be fate,* Virgil thought. He didn't know if he believed in fate, but it made sense. How else to explain such a coincidence? Never in eleven years had he seen Valencia Somerset outside of school, before today.

*"There are no coincidences."*

*"It's like you were meant to be friends."*

*"Anak?"* said Lola, pushing the cart forward a little as she considered the frozen pizzas. Joselito and Julius loved them, but Lola could never decide whether they were a good idea or not. "Cheap, but garbage," she said. "You off in la-la land?"

Valencia hadn't seen him. She was busy ignoring her mother. Virgil knew that ignoring-your-mother look.

What if she glanced up and saw him? Would she say hello? Should *he* say hello? How? How do you say hello to someone who has hearing aids? Do you talk like normal or do something special? He could wave, probably. But then what? What would he say after "hello"?

Virgil was suddenly very aware of his presence.

He casually stepped behind his grandmother. He couldn't let Valencia see him now. Not when he didn't know what to say or do. What if this was fate and he'd ruin it by being . . . well, himself?

"Sorry, Lola," Virgil muttered. "I was just thinking about something that happened on the last day of school."

Lola tossed the garbage pizza in the cart. "What? What happen?" She was always ready to hear gossip, no matter where it came from.

"Uh," said Virgil. "They served green beans at lunch."

Lola raised her eyebrows. "If that's your big news of the day, you really need to find more exciting things to do."

Lola pulled a bag of frozen Brussels sprouts out of the freezer and plopped them into the cart, too. She inched forward. There were only four people in the aisle now—them and the Somersets. Had the lights always been so bright in here?

It was difficult to stay hidden behind Lola. First of all, she was thin as a rail. Second of all, she turned around and said, "What you doing, Virgilio? *Ay sus*, you are right under my feet!"

Virgil stopped in his tracks.

Mrs. Somerset put a bag of frozen French fries in her cart. Valencia was still staring off into the freezer like it was the door to Narnia.

"Uh," said Virgil.

Fate had given him another chance and—what? He was going to hide behind his Lola?

He swallowed. "Uh," he said, again.

Any minute, Valencia would look up and see him, and then he'd have to do something. Say something.

*I'm going to do it. Right now. I'm going to wave or say hello. I don't care if I look stupid or not.*

*"There are no coincidences."*

He took a step forward.

When Valencia turned her back and walked

away without seeing him, he didn't know whether to laugh or cry.

He exhaled, defeated, and faced Lola. She was holding a bag of frozen peas in each hand, comparing prices or brands, Virgil didn't know which.

"Can we get ice cream?" he asked. The ice cream stood in neat rows in the opposite freezer. If he was going to be a failure, at least he could have something to look forward to. Quickly he added, "*Good* ice cream." Lola had a habit of picking the cheapest kind. It didn't make sense to Virgil. The brand she picked was three times bigger than other ice cream—it came in a big plastic tub—but it didn't taste very good. It seemed like more ice cream would cost more money, but apparently that's not how the world of ice cream worked. Virgil would rather have less if it tasted better.

Lola kept her eyes on the peas.

"Strawberry," she said.

Virgil would have preferred French vanilla, but he didn't want to press his luck.

He was scanning the ice cream, looking for the perfect kind—one with chunks of real, actual strawberries—when another familiar face appeared, reflected in the glass.

Chet Bullens, the Bull—pug-faced boy, as Lola would say, even though she'd never seen him with her own eyes—was right behind him, talking to his father.

It was as if there was a Boyd Middle School reunion at the Super Saver. The two people who ruled most of his thoughts were under this one industrial roof, right alongside two-for-one soda and bargain mangoes.

The Bull hadn't seen him. Not yet.

Virgil immediately opened the freezer. The door fogged quickly, obscuring Bull Junior and Bull Senior (but more importantly, obscuring *him*). He stood there until goose bumps erupted on his arms. Until his teeth rattled. Until he was sure the Bullens boys were gone and Lola called, from the end of the aisle, "Hurry up, *anak!*" He grabbed the container closest to him without even looking.

# 9
## Valencia

My name could lead people into battle.

*Valencia! Valencia! Valencia!*

Whether you think it or write it on paper, it's a good, strong name. The name of someone who enters a room and says "Here I am!" instead of "Where are you?"

Valencia Somerset—yes, it's a good name. Mom says they were going to name me Amy, but she took one look at me and saw Valencia.

My name is one of the only things that my mother and I agree on. Even right now. We're in the freezer aisle at the grocery store and she's reaching for the steak fries instead of the curly fries and, seriously? Who thinks steak fries are better?

I tap her on the shoulder so she's facing me and say, "Can't we get the curly kind?"

The buzz of the freezers hums in my hearing aids and drowns out most of her words, but I don't need to hear her clearly to know that she's saying no and talking about how I can buy whatever kind of fries I want when I'm older and have my own money for groceries, *blah blah blah*.

Whatever.

I didn't even want to come to the grocery store because it's boring and she never lets me get anything I want, but she said I had to come because my dad wasn't home from work yet and she needed help loading and unloading the groceries. There's no arguing with her, anyway. You never win—never. So now I'm here against my will, and I'm already grouchy because I had the nightmare again last night. I woke up with my heart pounding so hard I thought it would burst right out of my chest. I couldn't go back to sleep after that. So I've been awake since before dawn.

The only good thing about waking up before dawn is you get to see the sunrise. It happens slow and fast all at once, which is my favorite thing about it. You have to catch it at just the right time. If you do, you can watch the sky shift from gray to auburn and next thing you know, it's morning. No more darkness.

So I survived one nightmare, and now I'm stuck in another: the Super Saver with Mom.

"Go get me three avocados," she says, like I'm her personal servant. Then she gestures toward the produce section, which is like five hundred aisles away. Great. Now I have to find the avocados, and I don't even like them.

I decide to take my time. I walk super-slow and

think about all the cool things I could be doing instead of grocery shopping, like studying the bird's nest outside my parents' bedroom window. There are two baby birds inside. There used to be three. I pretend the third one went off on a fantastic journey somewhere, but I know better because I've read all about the nestling stage and I know how tough life can be for baby birds. It's hard to protect yourself when you can't fly. Sometimes they fall out of the nest. Sometimes another animal kidnaps and eats them. If I wasn't searching for avocados at the Super Saver, I could be at home watching over the other two birds, even though the tree is too high for me to reach them and I have to turn my head at a crazy angle to even get a peek. But still—at least they would know someone was watching over them. Like Saint Rene watches over me.

Even though I think avocados are weird and gross, I'm excellent at choosing the perfect ones. You have to pick an avocado that is darker in color, not too green. Then you place it in the palm of your hand and squeeze—gently, real gently. If you squeeze too hard, your avocado will get all bruised up. You want it to be soft but firm. If it squishes too much, it could be rotten. But if it squishes just a little, it's probably ripe and ready.

As soon as I have three perfect avocados, an announcement comes over the loudspeaker and roars in my hearing aids. Sometimes I think life is better when you can't hear all the noise. I can't make out every word, but I think I hear "specials of the week," which means it's going to be a five-hour-long announcement. I'm close to the automatic door, so I step through to get away from the sound, but then I remember I'm holding the avocados and I don't want to be a shoplifter so I stop where I am and look at this bulletin board near the entryway, like that was my plan the whole time.

The announcement stops as soon as I see something interesting.

Psychic?

No adults?

I didn't know there were psychics who only specialized in certain age groups.

I nibble at my bottom lip and stare at the words "PSYCHIC" and "NO ADULTS" for what seems like a hundred years. A thought forms in my head.

I know psychics focus on the future, but I don't care about my future. I'm worried about my right now. And right now, I'm sleep-deprived.

I yank off the card, get the number, and pull my

 66

phone out of my back pocket. I text the number one-handed, trying hard not to drop the avocados. I'm not as worried about my phone because my mom bought this super-protector so the screen wouldn't break if I dropped it. Except she said "when," not if—even though I've never broken anything in my whole life. Well, not that she knows of.

> Hi. just saw ur card at store. do u know anything ab dreams?

I wait. Right away, the word bubble pops up. She's typing.

> Yes. I know everything about dreams. I've studied Freud. Would you like an appointment?

Someone bumps into me, and I realize that I'm standing too close to the automatic doors. I take a step closer to the bulletin board. I'm just about to text back when it dawns on me that the person I'm texting could be a mass murderer or something. Just because the card says "Kaori Tanaka" doesn't mean the person is actually Kaori Tanaka. Or maybe the person *is* Kaori Tanaka, but Kaori Tanaka is an insane escaped madwoman who likes to eat eleven-year-olds for breakfast.

how old are u? how do I know ur not crazy killer?

I'm 12 and don't be ridiculous.

U dont sound 12.

The bubble appears again.

> That's because I'm the reincarnated spirit of a 65-year-old freedom fighter.

Hmm. I'm not sure if this makes me feel better or not.

I should give this some thought.

I slip the phone back into my pocket and walk toward the other end of the store to search for my mother. Along the way I see this scrunchy-faced boy from school. I think his name is Chet. The reason I know this is because Mr. Piper likes to write names on the board when kids act up, which is totally juvenile, but sometimes teachers treat us like we're seven years old. Teachers and parents have a lot in common.

Anyway, this boy's name is always on the

board because he acts like a complete moron most of the time. I don't know his last name, but it doesn't matter. I don't even think of him as Chet. I think of him as Scrunch. I know that's not very nice, but what can I say? His face is scrunched up, like he's sniffing something offensive. He's got beady eyes and round cheeks and they're all shoved up together. Meanness always shows on people's faces. Sometimes you have to look hard for it. Sometimes it's just a part of a person's features. That's how it is with this Chet.

So Scrunch is walking toward the checkout lanes with a grown-up Scrunch—his dad, I guess—as I'm walking in the opposite direction. I stare right at him as I walk by, because I already know something's coming. And it does. He sticks his fingers in both of his ears, crosses his eyes, and juts his tongue out of the side of his mouth. He's been doing this ever since the first day of school, when he realized I was deaf. He really needs to come up with new material.

"You're a doofus," I say.

I don't know if he hears me or not, but I don't care.

Let him hear.

# 10
## The Bullens Boys

There was something weird about being deaf. It wasn't natural. That girl had a lotta nerve.

Chet kind of suspected she wasn't really deaf, anyway. He wondered if she was just faking so she could spy on everyone. If she was deaf, how come she could talk? Even if it sounded like her mouth was full of marbles. She was probably faking that, too. Plus, she knew how to read lips, and that was just plain creepy. She probably read all their lips and kept a diary of their secrets. She probably knew everything, like who stole from the vending machine or carved curse words into the desks. And that made Chet's skin crawl, considering he was the one who did both of those things.

Chet looked up at his father. His dad had his "after-work look," as his mom called it—no tie, dress shirt unbuttoned at the collar, black slacks. Chet wasn't one hundred percent sure what his dad did at work, but whatever it was, Chet wanted to do it, too. Something about corporate sales, whatever that was. Something that made Mr. Bullens an important person who sometimes had to travel to faraway places like Europe or Seattle.

Mr. Bullens liked to say that a smart man had an answer for every question. That's how you get respect—you know more than anyone else and you teach people who aren't as smart as you. Respect came in two flavors, Mr. Bullens said: fear or admiration. Sometimes both. Otherwise you're just a weakling at the bottom of the food chain, ready to get crushed under someone else's boot.

That's why Chet liked asking his dad questions. He always got an answer. Learned something new.

"What makes people deaf?" Chet asked.

Mr. Bullens stopped and picked up a family-size bag of Doritos. Chet's dad loved Doritos. Sometimes he'd ask Chet to pick up a bag of chips for the house—any kind he wanted—and Chet always got Doritos, even though he secretly preferred Cheetos.

"Don't know. Lots of things, I guess," Mr. Bullens said, tossing the Doritos in the cart. "Some people are just born defective. Why? Do you see one?"

Chet casually glanced behind him. Valencia was gone. But he could still feel her glare.

There was definitely something wrong with that girl.

Deaf people were just weird, that's all.

"Nah," Chet said. "I was just wondering."

"They've got a few working here. Sometimes the grocery store gives jobs to those kind of people. Like a favor, you know? Disabled people don't have it all going on upstairs"—Mr. Bullens tapped his forehead—"but they can figure out how to bag groceries."

Chet nodded.

"I heard you outside banging the basketball on the driveway last night," Mr. Bullens said. They walked past the crackers and cookies. Mr. Bullens eyed everything without really looking at it. "Still practicing, huh?"

Chet felt his neck get warm. He hoped it wouldn't turn red.

"Yep. I figure if I practice all summer I might make the team this time. Tryouts aren't until fall, so . . ." Chet shrugged. Maybe if he played it casual, he'd look like it was no big deal. Fake it till you make it. He'd heard that somewhere.

Mr. Bullens said, "The coach isn't likely to forget the stink of last year's tryouts."

They moved out of the aisle. Mr. Bullens surveyed the checkout lines to find the shortest one. Chet followed closely behind.

"How many shots did you make last night?" his father asked.

Chet shoved his hands in his pockets and lumbered along more slowly as his father committed to cashier seven.

"A bunch," he said, clearing his throat. "I lost count."

Mr. Bullens turned to him and smiled widely. He patted Chet hard on the shoulder and pinched the back of his neck. "We can't all be basketball stars. You'll find your sport. It's just not on the court, that's all."

His father now turned his attention to the conveyer belt. The woman in front of them had it covered with frozen dinners, snack cakes, and two-liter sodas. The woman was large. Her house dress made her look even larger.

Mr. Bullens leaned toward his son and said, under his breath, "She oughta buy more vegetables, eh?" He laughed.

The woman glanced their way and gave them a snarling look, similar to the one Valencia had given Chet. He wondered if the woman had heard. He hoped she had. Sometimes the only way to teach people was to embarrass them, wake them up, make them see the error of their ways. That's what Mr. Bullens always said. It worked, too. People usually straightened up when Mr. Bullens was around.

Chet laughed. "Yeah," he said.

The woman had a lot of groceries, so it took awhile for the Bullens boys to unload their items. Hot dogs, Doritos, ground beef, ice-cream sandwiches, buttered popcorn, graham crackers, and two Hershey bars.

The teenage cashier was slow and fumbly, with a face full of pimples. His name was

Kenny, according to his name tag, which hung crookedly off his shirt pocket. Underneath it said TRAINEE.

"By the time we get out of here, my son'll be graduating from high school," said Mr. Bullens.

He laughed to show he was only joking.

"More like college," Chet added, loud enough so only his dad could hear.

# 11
## Beware the Color Red

Guinea pigs don't have normal sleeping schedules. Virgil learned this from the internet. They were small and weak—easy for other animals to snatch up and eat—so they had to be prepared at all times. That didn't leave much time for restful sleep; instead, guinea pigs like Gulliver slept in fits and starts, in fifteen-minute intervals. Virgil could never really tell when Gulliver was sleeping, since his eyes were always open and he spent a lot of time hiding in his plastic tree hut.

That's not to say Gulliver was quiet. Even though he still held on to his instinctual ways, he was comfortable enough that he ventured around the cage and made quite a bit of noise. He liked to rattle his water bottle, for one thing. That's what woke Virgil up at seven o'clock on Saturday morning.

*Rattle, rattle. Rattle, rattle.*

"Ugh, Gulliver," Virgil mumbled. He threw the blankets over his head, but it was no use. He was awake for good.

Maybe it was for the best. Now he could enjoy breakfast, get Gulliver packed, and have plenty of time to find the five stones. He wondered for about the zillionth time what Kaori planned to do with them. Maybe she'd use them to pelt him in the head so he could stop doing things like hiding behind freezer doors at the Super Saver.

He got up, stretched, and opened his bedroom door. He listened. All was quiet. Good.

He walked on the balls of his feet down the hall, careful not to make any noise so he wouldn't wake anyone up. For his sake, not theirs. His parents and brothers were a lot to take at any time of the day, but especially in the morning.

The whole house was quiet.

It was marvelous.

Virgil was so overjoyed at the stillness of his usually bustling house that he didn't even glance at the kitchen table as he opened the refrigerator. He was too busy relishing in the discovery that he could hear his thoughts. No one talking loud or laughing louder. No one calling him Turtle.

He reached for the milk. The morning was off to a glorious start. He'd sit quietly and have his Cinnamon Toast Crunch and consider the day ahead. He'd think about finding five stones, each of a different size, in the woods near Kaori's house. He wasn't supposed to go exploring in the woods, but he knew that was the best place to find good stones. Sure, he could have stolen some out of the garden in the back, but for some reason that didn't feel right. Like it didn't count. He wasn't sure Kaori would approve of garden stones.

"You're using too much milk."

Virgil jumped. A splash of milk missed his cereal and landed with a splat on the counter.

It was Lola, reading a magazine at the kitchen table.

"You scared me," said Virgil.

"You should always survey a room when you enter it," Lola replied. "Take a good look around. Never be caught off guard."

"I was busy thinking." Virgil wiped up the spill, returned the milk to the fridge, and carried his bowl to the table. Lola was right; he'd used too much milk. The bowl was filled to the brim.

Lola put down her magazine and narrowed her eyes. "You've been doing a lot of thinking lately. What's going on in that brain of yours?

And don't tell me more green-bean stories."

Virgil paused. He wouldn't tell her about Valencia. He wasn't ready. This was one thing he didn't want her advice on.

But it certainly wouldn't hurt to get her thoughts on a few other things.

Virgil took a heaping bite of cereal and said, "Do you believe in fate?"

Lola sat back. "Oh, yes," she said. "Certainly I do."

"So you believe things happen for a reason?"

"*Ay sus.* Don't talk with your mouth full. And yes, I do. I think good things happen for a reason. And bad things, too."

Virgil swallowed. "Why do you always bring up the bad things?"

"If you didn't have bad things, you wouldn't have good things. They would all just be things. Did you ever think about that?"

"No." Virgil looked at his cereal. "I guess not."

"I believe in signs, too, Virgilio." She raised her

eyebrow, like she was harboring a deep secret.

"What kind of signs?"

Lola leaned forward. "Last night, I had a dream about a boy named Amado. He was walking through a meadow when he saw a bright red tree. He was so mesmerized by this tree that he decided to walk to it, even though everyone told him not to. 'No, no,' they said. 'Don't go, Amado. The tree is bad. Very bad.' But Amado didn't listen. He had never seen a tree like it. On he went." She pressed her fingertip to the tabletop, as if Amado was standing right there. "There he goes, ignoring everybody, and do you know what happen?"

Virgil lifted a spoonful of milk to his lips and slurped. "The tree ate him?"

"Yes. Exactly." She leaned back in her chair again. "So you know what the sign is, Virgilio?"

"Don't walk up to trees when people say not to?"

"No. Beware the color red."

"Beware the color red?"

"Just for today." She pointed to Virgil. "That's my advice to you today. You remember, Virgilio, yes?"

"Yes, Lola," said Virgil, before scooping another spoonful. "I'll remember."

# 12
## Valencia

There is a special light in the hallway that blinks when someone rings the doorbell. This morning I wake up and see it flashing through my half-open bedroom door. I'm not sure what kind of sadist rings doorbells at seven thirty on a Saturday morning, but I'm going to find out because I'm the only one awake. I can tell by the way the house feels. Like even the walls are asleep.

I walk down the hall in my bare feet. I don't

bother with my hearing aids. A man with a salt-and-pepper mustache and a girl with brown eyes and freckles are at the door. They have pamphlets tucked under their arms. I can tell they aren't lost. They look like they are just where they need to be, which is strange because I've never seen them before. The man says hello and introduces the both of them, but his mustache makes it hard for me to understand him. I think his name is Craig or Greg, and her name is something indecipherable with an *E*, maybe. Something that doesn't make you move your lips, like Enid.

Before he and his mustache go on any further, I point to my ear and shake my head to show that I'm deaf, and he looks at me like I just sprouted vines from my head. Then he hands me a pamphlet in a big hurry, and he and the freckled girl step away from the door and wave good-bye. He moves his mouth in such an exaggerated way that I can see all his teeth when he says "Nice to meet you," which is really easy to lip read because everyone says it. I can tell he's saying it really loudly, as if that would make a difference. As they walk away, the girl turns and looks at me like I'm a zoo exhibit. I think about sticking my tongue out at her, but I don't. They're going to have a rude awakening anyway because they're headed next door to Mrs. Franklin's house, and she doesn't like when people come by unannounced. Plus Mrs. Franklin has three cats, and they're the meanest cats you ever saw. I have a feeling those cats would claw that man's mustache off if Mrs. Franklin told them to.

I close the door and look at that pamphlet. It looks like something for church. On the outside it says, in great big letters, ONLY THOSE WHO LISTEN TO THE WORD CAN HEAR IT. That's kinda funny, all things considered. But it's really a shame that Greg/Craig didn't stay to talk to me, because I bet there aren't many people who would be willing to listen, especially since they're going around ringing doorbells at seven thirty on a Saturday morning. I would have listened, though.

Had they stayed, I would have asked all about their church and what kinds of things they do and I would have asked if they thought God was a boy or a girl or an old man with a white beard and I would have asked if they knew about Saint Rene and if they didn't, I would have told them. And maybe I could've made them coffee because I know how. And I would have asked what time their church services started and if they baptize people and if so, how?

But instead I'm staring at the pamphlet like an idiot. I toss it in the kitchen trash because I know neither of my parents will care.

My dad comes down the hallway. He's scratching the back of his neck the way he always does when he first wakes up.

"Who was at the door, cupcake?" I can tell that's what he says, because it's a logical question and he always calls me cupcake. I should probably hate it because it's a babyish nickname, but I hope he calls me cupcake even when I'm really old, like thirty.

"Church people," I say. I pull the pamphlet out of the trash and show it to him. He rolls his eyes.

"What do you plan to do today?" he asks. Then he yawns and walks toward the pantry. He's going to make himself a bowl of cereal. That's what he does every morning. Sometimes he even eats cereal for dinner. No one eats more cereal than my dad. And he likes the real sugary kind, the ones that make your teeth rot, at least according to my mom. For some reason it really irritates her that he eats so much cereal. She says it's not real food.

"I'm going out to explore with my zoological diary," I say.

I don't mention the part about going to see Kaori.

Turns out, my need to find a cure for nightmares outweighs my fear of maniacs. I've decided to take my chances. My appointment is at one o'clock.

One sharp, actually. Apparently Kaori Tanaka is very serious about being on time, which makes me think maybe she's not a killer. I don't think punctuality would be number one on her list of worries if she was.

For added protection, I didn't give her my real identity. When she asked, I told her my name was Renee. She asked for my last name, but I said, "It's just Renee." I couldn't think of a fake last name fast enough.

I return to my room as my dad pours milk over his Cap'n Crunch. Maybe I'll fall back to sleep. It's still early, and I'm not ready to be awake.

I shake my Crystal Caverns globe, then get under the covers before the bats settle back down in the water.

Kaori told me she lives on the other side of the woods. That's good news, because it's not far. Otherwise I don't know how I would make it to her house. It's also great luck because I know the woods like the back of my hand. I know there's a special clearing where groundhogs come out at dusk. I know there's an old abandoned water well that's missing its rope and pail, which tells me that the woods used to be an empty field where someone had a house, which means that the trees are young, as least as far as trees go. There are sycamore, pin oaks, and poplars. I know there's a cluster of trees with leaves that turn brilliant shades of yellow in the fall. It's one of my favorite places, and it's where I do most of my journaling. I've even walked through the whole length of it and come out the other side, into a neighborhood. Maybe I've even seen Kaori's house before. You never know.

She should put a sign in her yard or something. Drum up more business.

I close my eyes and think about that pamphlet. I wonder where Mustache's church is. I wish I'd asked him.

Oh, well. I can pretend I'm in a church.

I imagine that I'm sitting in a pew—would Mustache's church have pews or chairs?—and looking up at a big, big altar, talking to Saint Rene. He doesn't look at me like I have vines sprouting from my head, because he understands. I try to picture Saint Rene wearing hearing aids in both ears like I do.

"Dear Saint Rene," I say. "I've been thinking about that whole going-solo thing and I'm not sure it's the best idea after all. It'd be nice if I didn't have to go to Kaori Tanaka's house alone, just in case she eats eleven-year-olds for breakfast. I didn't have the nightmare last night, which is good because I need to be alert. Kaori may or may not be a mass murderer. If she is, please protect me. Thank you. Amen. I'm not sure if I'm supposed to say amen or not, but it sounds good. So. Amen."

# 13
## Snakes

Chet woke up on Saturday morning thinking about snakes. John Davies claimed that he had found a snakeskin in the woods near the school, and Chet planned to one-up him. He wouldn't just find *snakeskin*. He'd capture an actual *snake*.

He knew just how he would do it too. He'd find a good, long stick. Then he'd look for places where snakes hang out, like in the brush or tall grass or something. And he'd poke around until he heard one move. He'd poke and poke and poke—standing at a distance, of course; he wasn't stupid—until the snake raised its head and hissed, or whatever snakes did. And as soon as it lifted up off the ground to attack him, he would snatch it by its tail so he wouldn't get bit, then grab it under the head, as fast as possible, with his other hand. He was quick. Quicker than a snake, that's for sure. And he wasn't scared either.

Today would be the day. It was meant to be.

His favorite thing about snakes was how they swallowed their prey with one giant gulp. People were afraid of snakes, too, but that just showed how cowardly people were. Not Chet, though. At last year's field trip, he had held a boa constrictor without a second thought, even though Miss Bosch and the keeper of the reptile house, Mr. Frederick, said it could crush bones just by squeezing.

"You're all cowards," Chet had announced to everyone in earshot. "Scared of a little ol' snake."

David Kistler crossed his arms. "Doesn't look little to me," he said.

"Figures you'd be scared of it, *Kiss*ler," said Chet. "You can't even run ten steps without dropping dead."

David was a short kid with asthma who always carried an inhaler.

Chet puffed out his chest and continued, "Besides, it won't hurt me. He knows who's boss."

Chet's arms began to ache from the weight. He didn't let on, but he also didn't argue when Mr. Frederick reached over to return the snake to its tank. That was when the Valencia girl had raised her hand. She had a lotta nerve asking questions, Chet thought.

When Mr. Frederick called on her, she asked, "Can snakes hear?"

The class snickered, Chet included.

David shot everyone a mean look and said, "Shut up" to no one in particular. Everyone did.

Even Chet, but only because Mr. Frederick was about to start talking again.

A kid the size of a first grader who sucked on an inhaler all the time sure had a lotta nerve shushing people, Chet thought.

Mr. Frederick made a seesaw motion with his hand as if to say "so-so."

"Excellent question," said Mr. Frederick. "Snakes don't have ears, but they can hear through vibrations in the skin. The vibrations travel to the inner ear, and that's how the snake hears the sound. It's not the same kind of sounds that you or I hear, though. Scientists aren't sure what it actually sounds like."

Figures she would ask a question about ears when she didn't have any that worked, Chet thought. Then again, she probably wore those big hearing aids just to get extra attention. She didn't even try to hide them, which only proved his point. Plus, she spent Thursday afternoons in the resource room, which was way easier than regular class. On the other days of the week, the teachers wore microphones that worked with her hearing aids somehow. Talk about special treatment. And the teachers never called on her or asked her to come up to the board to solve problems unless she raised her hand. Meanwhile, they hounded Chet. "Come sit up front." "Stop that." "Leave that kid alone." "Where's your homework?" This Valencia girl was nothing more than a con artist.

Chet watched her as she eyed the boa constrictor. Maybe she used the hearing aids to tune in to some other world and she was a witch, or she practiced voodoo at home or something. Maybe she spoke to people and animals with her mind. There was something off about the whole thing.

When the class filed out, Valencia stayed behind, studying the snake, and no one even told her to move. Not even Mr. Frederick. It was like she was invisible.

That girl got away with everything.

# 14
## The Universe Knows

Petty items like furniture crowded the spirit chamber, so Kaori kept it sparse. Her parents forced her to have a bed, but she convinced them to banish the dresser to the garage. Her closet was overstuffed, but it was worth it. The extra space allowed her to examine the star chart from various angles, which was exactly what she was doing at eight o'clock Saturday morning after nudging her sister out of bed. There was important business to consider: how does one unite a Pisces and Scorpio without interfering with the destiny of the stars? This was a delicate matter. It was one thing to use the existing magnetic forces of fate. It was another to manipulate the universe to do your bidding.

She needed a plan.

"The stars are aligned in their favor," Kaori said. She stood in front of the star chart with her shoulders squared, feet apart, hands on her hips.

"How can you tell?" Gen asked. She was standing the same way, only her pajama bottoms were inside-out and she had the jump rope looped around her waist like a sash. "Looks like nothing but a bunch of dots and lines."

Kaori sighed. "I've told you a million times. The dots are stars and the lines are the constellations. And it's not *lines*, in the first place. It's pictures. See? This is Orion. The three stars are his belt. He's hunting. Can't you tell?"

Gen tilted her head to the right, then the left. "Looks like lines."

"And this is Andromeda and Pegasus. See?" Kaori indicated points on the star chart.

"Yeah, I can see because they have names written right next to them. But it still looks like lines."

Kaori sighed again. "Forgive her," she said, to the spirits.

"How is this supposed to help us figure out what to do?"

"The stars tell us everything. It's fate, Gen. Fate in the stars. There are no coincidences."

Gen squinted at the chart. "Is my fate in there?"

"Sure. Your fate is to help me figure out what to do."

"I thought Virgil was just gonna bring us some rocks and we were gonna do abracadabra stuff."

"Stones, not rocks."

"That's the same thing."

"Not really."

"What's the difference, then?"

Kaori rubbed her head. "It's just different. Geez. Can't you let me think? You have no idea what we're up against, bringing these two signs together."

"Maybe they weren't meant to be friends. Just because they have the same initials doesn't mean anything. I have the same initials as Gertrude Tomlinson and I don't like her at all. She broke three of my pink glitter pencils and didn't even apologize. And she chewed off the erasers, which is totally gross."

"They're meant to be friends. It's fate. I know it," Kaori said. "Somehow the universe figures these things out."

"How?"

"Like putting them in the same place at the same time, or using a special force like me to help them find their way."

"They were in the same place at the same time for a whole year at school, and they didn't even speak."

"That was Virgil, not the universe. You can see how shy he is. He carries a rodent in his backpack, Gen. A *rodent*."

"It's not a rodent. It's a guinea pig."

"That's what guinea pigs are. They're rodents. Just like rats or squirrels or mice."

"I think Gulliver's cute."

"I'm just saying. It can't be easy for Virgil. First off, he's a Pisces." Kaori turned away from the star chart and walked to the edge of her circle rug. Gen followed at her heels. "Look at the sign for Pisces. It's two fish swimming in opposite directions. Do you know why?"

Gen shook her head.

"Because Pisces are always at odds with themselves. They're never quite sure what to do. No self-confidence. Overly sensitive."

Gen squatted down to get a good look at the fish.

"Now look at Scorpio," Kaori said.

Gen's dark eyes shifted to the neighboring sign on the rug. "Ew. It's a bug."

"No," Kaori snapped, as if Gen had just cursed both their parents. "Well, yes. It's a bug. But not just any bug. It's a scorpion, Gen. A *scorpion*. Do you know what that means?"

"She has a tail?"

Kaori apologized to the spirits again, then said, "No. It means she's sharp and independent. She's assertive, full of confidence. She's probably got a little temper, too, and a ton of friends, all competing for her attention, while poor Virgil talks to a rodent. Basically, they're the exact opposite of each other. Nothing in common, I bet. Not a thing."

Gen considered this. She looked up at her sister. "Maybe she likes rodents, too."

Kaori sighed for a third time.

"Don't be ridiculous," she said.

# 15
## Valencia

Squirrels are one of my favorite animals. I decide that's going to be my focus today as I cross the woods. I'm going to study the squirrels and feed Sacred, my pet dog.

Okay, he's not really my dog. But he may as well be. I take care of him more than anyone else, I guarantee you that. He could be my pet if my parents weren't so anti-dog. They claim they aren't, but they refuse to let me bring Sacred home because they say pets are a big responsibility and they don't want to be the ones taking care of him. I tell them the whole point is that he would be my pet, which means I would take care of him, but they don't listen. They don't think I'm responsible enough to take care of a dog, but how would they know? We've never had one. I think they just don't want a dog in the house. If that's the case, they should just say so instead of blaming the whole thing on my perceived lack of responsibility. I don't get them sometimes, I really don't.

So because my parents think I don't know how to feed or walk a dog, Sacred is stuck out there in the woods, fending for himself. I take good care of him. I bring him a bowl of food every time I go animal watching, and he always shows up. He's the sweetest dog. You wouldn't know it to look at him—not at first. He's a big dog and he looks mean because he's kinda mangy. I mean, he lives by his wits in the woods, so he isn't exactly wagging his tail twenty-four hours a day. But all I had to do was look at his face, and I knew he was friendly. You know how I said meanness shows up in people's faces? It's the same for dogs, too. It's the same for all animals who have eyes. Most of the time.

Sacred is all black. For some reason people are more afraid of black dogs than dogs of any other color. Now that I think about it, it's the same for cats, too. I don't know why. Dogs and cats can't exactly control the color of their fur, so why does it make a difference if they're born with black fur or brown fur? It's all hair. People are weird sometimes, I swear.

I decide to head into the woods around ten thirty. That will give me plenty of time to document squirrel activity in my log, feed Sacred, and get to Kaori's house without rushing. But first I need to swipe a bowl from the kitchen. Every now and then my parents have Styrofoam or plastic bowls on hand, but most of the time they don't, so I have to secretly take a real one. I always pick the ones my parents don't use so they won't notice, but lately Mom's been going through the cabinets and I think she suspects something. I can see her mind wondering, *What happened to my bowls?*

Here's the thing: every time I bring Sacred food in the woods, I plan to return the bowl, wash it, and put it back in the cabinet. No one is the wiser, right? But every now and then (okay, most of the time), Sacred brings the bowl to an undisclosed location, never to be seen again. I know I need a better plan, but I always forget to come up with one, and I don't think about it until I'm about to feed Sacred—like right now, for instance.

I make a mental note. *Figure out a more creative way to bring food.*

Maybe I could build a dog feeder and nail it to a tree.

But there's no time for that now.

I wait until my parents are in the den watching

Saturday morning news—which is totally boring and has the worst closed captioning, by the way—and I snatch one of the bowls in a big hurry. I fill it up with corn flakes, five slices of bologna, one slice of cheese, and a handful of baby carrots. I know it doesn't sound very appetizing. Trust me, it doesn't look appetizing either. But Sacred isn't picky.

When you're hungry, you're hungry.

Unfortunately, I'm not able to make a simple escape. My mother tugs my shirt before I can get out the door.

"Where are you going with that?" she asks.

"Outside for breakfast."

She looks inside the bowl and raises an eyebrow. "That's what you're eating for breakfast?"

"Uhh . . . yes?"

Okay, I know I'm not very convincing. But if I tell her I'm going into the woods to feed a stray dog, she'll freak out. She tends to freak out over the dumbest things.

"Then I'm going exploring." I turn sideways so she can see the small bag over my shoulder, which carries my journal (aka my zoological diary) and favorite sketching pencil.

She considers this, and I consider her.

Did I catch her on a good day, or is she going to be a big pain?

"Be careful," she says. "And be back by the afternoon. Don't wander too far, either."

My mom is like a walking list of dos and don'ts.

"Got it," I say.

"I love you. Keep your phone on."

There's always a footnote to her *I love you*s. "I love you, be home by four." "I love you, be sure to answer my texts." "I love you, be careful."

I wonder if she does it to my dad, too.

"Love you, too, Mom. And I will," I say as I walk out the door.

I guess I use footnotes, too.

# 16
## Down, Down, Down

Of all the treats in the entire world—celery sticks, baby carrots, orange slices—Gulliver liked dandelions best. It took him less than five seconds to eat an entire stem, and then he'd root around for more. For Gulliver, dandelions were a rare delicacy. For humans, they were noxious weeds that needed to stop growing. But grow they did. Dandelions were everywhere in Virgil's neighborhood. They sprouted from the cracks in the sidewalk, leaned against rusty fence posts, sneaked into well-manicured lawns. Virgil plucked them habitually, like an explorer searching for gems. By the time he reached the woods, his left pocket was stuffed with them. He could have stuffed the other pocket, too, but he was saving that for the stones.

He wasn't allowed to explore the woods alone. The trees were thick in some places and sparse in others. Flowers grew intermittently; a patch of iris here, a colony of dandelions there. Lola was convinced the woods teemed with snakes, but Virgil was certain that he could find five stones here. And not just any stones, but the best stones his town had to offer.

He found two right away, just a few feet into the woods. Deeper in, the sounds of the neighborhood faded away and he found another, just like that. He was so focused on looking down, surveying the ground with his eyes, that he barely noticed the ominous rustling sound behind him. But when he heard the shuffle of feet, he jerked around—heart pounding—and stood very, very still. If there was one thing he knew, it was that you had to stay still when faced with forest beasts. Otherwise you could become their supper.

He didn't see anything. But he was certain he had heard something. And it wasn't the blowing of the wind or the falling of a twig. Someone—or something—was moving nearby.

"Hello?" Virgil said, quietly, like a croak.

He thought he heard something. A growl? A snort? He suddenly got the idea that there was a rhinoceros on the other side of the trees, pawing its front hoof in the dirt, bowing its head, steadying its horn, ready to charge. He imagined himself being flung into the air and landing on the thick gray skin of the giant creature before being trampled. One of Lola's old ghost stories popped into his head, too. She said there was once a man who told all his secrets to the trees, and after he died, the trees whispered them to anyone who passed by. Maybe it wasn't a rhinoceros, but a bunch of old trees that were ready to tell the secrets of the dead.

Virgil looked at his phone. It was ten fifteen. Maybe he'd just snatch up the next stones he saw and rush to Kaori's house. She might not mind if he got there early.

But then the shuffling sound receded and disappeared, and the woods were quiet again. Virgil exhaled. His heart slowed. He looked at his feet, saw a fourth stone, and put it in his pocket. He wondered if he'd picked the best ones. He wondered so deeply that he didn't hear the other shuffling sound, this time approaching from behind.

"Hey, retardo."

Virgil turned around, startled.

Chet Bullens's meaty face was a light shade of red, like it was ready to burst. "What're you doing out here all by yourself? Lost your mommy?"

It occurred to Virgil that the Bull was also out here by himself, but he wasn't about to point that out. Instead, Virgil said nothing. He stood there, one pocket full of stones and the other full of dandelions, feeling very dumb, like someone had lifted him out of one story and placed him in another, in these unfamiliar woods in this unfamiliar situation—alone with the Bull, who was carrying a pillowcase. Virgil wondered what the pillowcase was for, and in the space of about three seconds, he thought of a handful of terrifying scenarios: the Bull would smother him with it. He was using it to carry the bodies of dead animals. He was going to capture animals, smother them, then carry their dead bodies.

And Chet wasn't just carrying a pillowcase. He was also wearing a Chicago Bulls T-shirt.

*"Beware the color red."*

Suddenly the rhinoceros didn't seem so bad.

"Whatsa matter?" the Bull said. "Oh, yeah, I forgot. You don't know how to talk. You're a retard.

I see you going into that retard class all the time. What goes on in there, anyways? A bunch of kids wetting their pants, I bet."

In addition to being afraid of the dark, carrying a guinea pig in his backpack, and stuffing his pockets full of dandelions and rocks, Virgil had another secret: he weighed only seventy-six pounds, and even though he pretended to be five feet tall, he was actually four foot eleven.

Virgil wasn't sure how much the Bull weighed or how tall he was, but he certainly weighed more than seventy-six pounds.

"You really are stupid, huh?" the Bull said. His eyes shifted to Virgil's backpack.

Chet took a step forward and Virgil took a step back, which the Bull thought was hilarious, because he immediately broke into peals of laughter before ripping Virgil's backpack off his shoulders with such force that Virgil spun—actually spun—and hit the ground with a numbing whack that shot from the palms of his hands to his shoulders. The Bull took off like a bullet; Virgil pushed himself up and ran after him, saying, "No! No! No!" in the loudest voice he could manage without choking.

"Gulliver! Gulliver!" he cried. Or maybe he only said it in his head. He wasn't sure.

The Bull darted between the trees, not laughing anymore, just running with Virgil's backpack in his hands. A million horrifying images blazed through Virgil's mind—the Bull tearing Gulliver in two, feeding him to a pit of lions, picking him up and tossing him into the trees—which is why he didn't feel any better when the Bull finally stopped running and turned to face him, his cheeks flushed and his neck and hairline glistening.

Virgil waited for him to open the backpack, discover Gulliver, and destroy him. Instead the Bull took a giant step back, grinned evilly, and turned toward a stumpy circle of stones that Virgil had never noticed before.

It was an old well.

With two hefty shoves, the Bull pushed the cover of the well aside and dangled the backpack over the now-open hole.

"Say bye-bye to your stuff, retardo," he said.

The Bull let go, and the bag fell into the dark, gaping well, so far down that Virgil didn't even hear it land.

"Guess you'll have to get new books, pansy boy," the Bull said, his smile widening. "Not that you need them anyway, since you probably don't know how to read."

The Bull wiped his hands on the front of his jeans as if he'd just finished a dirty, dirty deed— which he had. And then he turned and walked away, disappearing into the woods and leaving Virgil alone.

# 17
## Going Underground

There are more than seven thousand islands in the Philippines. Some don't even have people living on them. And then there are some that once had people, but don't anymore. Like the lowland island of Balatama. Lola had told Virgil all about it.

According to Lola, Balatama was once a thriving island in the south. It thrived so much that the people kept taking, taking, taking land that belonged to the mountain creatures. One day the people cut down a gathering of trees that belonged to a majestic bird named Pah.

Pah had the wingspan of an elephant and talons as sharp as knives. When his trees were cut down, he was so angry that he grew bigger and bigger. When he spread his wings, they were so large and dark that they blotted out the sunlight. This made Pah happy because the darkness blinded the villagers. They would get lost and wander in circles and then Pah would swoop down, pluck them up, and eat them.

Pah controlled the darkness and used it as a weapon. He knew that darkness turned people weak because it confused them and made them wander. The darkness created easy victims because no one could fight an enemy they could not see. Pah's talons would sever the villagers in half before they even realized they were in trouble.

Virgil was eight years old the first time he heard the story of Pah. Now, as he leaned over the side of the well, he half expected Pah's talons to come shooting out of it. Even though it was a bright sunny afternoon aboveground, the deep well that now cradled Gulliver was a dark, dark place. And darkness was *darkness*, whether it was in the sky or not.

Virgil's heart thundered in his ears. A tight knot collected in his chest and rose, rose, rose until it pushed its way to his eyes, which pooled with tears.

"Gulliver?" he said.

The inky blackness gaped up at him, like the throat of a hungry beast. It smelled musty and dank and deathly. But Gulliver was down there. He couldn't leave Gulliver—not for a second.

There was hope, though.

A ladder.

He had no choice.

He emptied his pocket of the stones and set them carefully on the rim of the well.

Then he started his journey down.

The descent was unsteady. Virgil's foot hesitated

before every rung, but ultimately landed—quivering—where it belonged. With each step he gripped the ladder tighter and tighter until his knuckles ached. Down, down, down. Was the bottom of the well full of water? Was Gulliver drowning, struggling to breathe? So deep and black was the well that Virgil couldn't see anything, not even when he was six rungs down, and for a moment he thought that maybe he'd descended for nothing; maybe the Bull hadn't thrown Gulliver inside after all, and he'd just imagined the whole thing.

But then, after what seemed like forever, there it was. Not floating in water, but slouched on its side at the bottom of the well, zipper still open just an inch, just enough for Gulliver to breathe. The darkness had invaded Virgil's lungs and choked him, and he couldn't breathe until he knew Gulliver was breathing, too. He listened for him—chuttering, chirping, *anything*—but all he heard was the drumming of his own heart.

Virgil was still a fair distance from the bottom when he lowered his foot and discovered there was no longer a rung for him to step onto. He clutched the rusty bars and craned his neck to look down, slowly, slowly, so as not to lose his balance, and realized he'd reached the end of the ladder, but he needed two more rungs. At least. The backpack wasn't within reach—not even close—and his legs weren't long enough to touch the ground.

Virgil could see the backpack. He couldn't tell if there was any movement inside, but he certainly couldn't just climb back out and give up. Not without Gulliver. The thought of abandoning Gulliver was far worse than the realization that he'd have to jump.

He pulled himself closer to the ladder—hugging it almost, chest to iron, as if the mere thought of jumping would send him falling to his death. And now he heard his own breathing. It broke through the silence in quick, rapid spurts, like the hiccups.

All at once, he began to sweat. A faucet inside of him turned on and everything dampened: the insides of his elbows, the palms of his hands, the space between each of his perfectly shaped fingers, the back of his neck, each hairlined follicle of his forehead, his size-five feet, the space between his shoulder blades. Everything.

If this was how the body prepared to jump, he thought, it wasn't very useful.

He lowered his right foot and pressed the toe of his sneaker against the well, then brought his right hand down to the next iron bar. He stayed like that for several moments, unsure what to do, looking like two halves of one boy—one climbing down, the other going up. He didn't lower his left hand until his legs started to ache, and he didn't move his other foot until he absolutely had to. When he did, he was hanging from the third-to-last rung like they were monkey bars, which he'd never been able to cross in his entire life.

He went down to the next bar and pointed his toe, to see if he felt the ground yet.

Nothing.

He lowered himself again. Again.

Now he dangled from the ladder with nowhere else to go but down. He had to let go, but he couldn't. A dozen images fired through his brain. He saw himself clutching a broken arm and wailing in pain. He saw twisted ankles with the bones sticking out. A head injury that left him motionless until he finally evaporated into a skeleton. A bloody gash above his eyebrow as he slammed against the well's rugged walls.

These all seemed likely scenarios, what with the distance to the bottom.

But there was Gulliver.

"Gulliver," said Virgil. He expected his voice to echo, but it didn't.

He looked up. The mouth of the well was a perfect circle above him. There was daylight there.

And air. There were trees and birds and Lola. The well smelled like an old sock. The world smelled like trees and grass. He looked up, at the light. He looked down, at Gulliver.

He let go.

There are many terrible things that can happen to a boy who jumps into a well. He could break his head open, suffer a broken arm, twist his ankles, bones sticking out, all that. Or his cell phone could fall out of his pocket and shatter into a million pieces.

Virgil's phone and his feet hit about a half second apart. As soon as he felt the ground under his sneakers and the numb tingling of pain from impact, he realized two things: he had landed safely, and his phone had not. But the first thing he did was grab his backpack and zip it open.

He reached in to feel Gulliver and heard a single, healthy chirp. Gulliver was none the wiser—he just wanted a dandelion, so Virgil gave him one.

"You're okay," Virgil said, even though Gulliver already knew this.

Virgil's heart had been a steady drumbeat in his ears, but it quelled now. He rested the backpack against the wall and reached for his phone.

It had broken into three pieces—screen, battery, and everything else. Virgil put the pieces back together, because you don't give up without trying, Lola always said.

"All the king's horses and all the king's men . . . ," said Virgil, snapping the battery in place. It fit fine, but he could see already that there was no hope for the screen. There was a crack in the corner that branched out like a spiderweb. "Couldn't put Humpty together again."

He tried to turn it on, but nothing happened. He tried again. He shook it, he took it apart again and put it back together, he kept his thumb on the power button until it hurt. Nothing.

He put the phone in his pocket anyway. Then

he tipped his head back and looked up, up, up. The light was there, but it was far away, like a cloud he couldn't touch.

He stood under the ladder. He reached toward the bottom rung, but his fingertips were nowhere near it. He got on his tiptoes, so high that it hurt, but he still couldn't reach. He bent his knees and jumped with all his might, arms outstretched, and that didn't do any good either.

*If I were Joselito or Julius, I would have no trouble reaching the ladder,* he thought. *But then again, if I were Joselito or Julius, I wouldn't be down here in the first place.*

He jumped again.

He looked toward the light.

"Hello?" he said, hesitant at first. "Hello?" Then, louder: "Hello? Hello? Hello?"

He knew it wouldn't do any good. No one was ever out in the woods. And even if they were, they probably couldn't hear him.

# 18
## Animal

Chet was now convinced that Davies had lied about the snakeskin. He hadn't found the first bit of evidence that there were any snakes in the woods. Then again, he wasn't exactly sure what kind of evidence snakes left behind besides snakeskin—but nonetheless, he hadn't found any. He'd even broken off a branch so he could root around. He used the branch to push aside clusters of fallen twigs and small bunches of leaves, to see if a snake was hiding underneath, fangs at the ready. And he wasn't even scared, either. Because he was no chicken.

The noises in the woods were fairly standard— the occasional tweet of some stupid bird, the faraway sound of a car driving down a road in the neighborhood, the sound of Chet's sneakers hitting the ground—but during a particularly detailed search at the base of an ash tree, while Chet diligently poked at the ground with his branch, he heard something different. It sounded like someone moving stealthily through the trees. Someone or something.

He half expected to come face-to-face with a grizzly bear, but then he realized how ridiculous that was.

He reminded himself that he was no chicken, even though his heart was pounding.

When he didn't see anything, he stood up straighter and turned all the way around to give the area a proper survey. He listened. He heard it again, now from another direction. The shifting, the movement. He shifted, too—quickly. So quickly that he made a lot of noise.

"Shhh," he said to himself.

He raised the branch, prepared to use it as a weapon.

"Who's there?" he said, but his voice was so quiet and whispery that he wasn't sure anyone would've heard it.

Then it dawned on him: It was probably that idiot boy with the backpack. The skinny kid who never talked. The Chinese or whatever-he-was kid. He was probably trying to make his way back home and wanted to stay out of sight. Which made perfect sense, all things considered. Let's face it, that kid was no match for Chet Bullens.

Chet's confidence returned. It bloomed through his body until his shoulders relaxed and his chest puffed out.

"Hey, dumbo," he said. "Is that you? Sneaking off to the bookstore?"

Chet laughed like this was the funniest thing he'd said all day. He often thought he would make a good comedian, what with all his funny jokes.

Chet waited. His eyes moved slowly from tree to tree. The thought of someone being so afraid that he had to sneak by made Chet feel like a warlord or warrior. Sometimes before he went to bed at night he even imagined himself that way—like it was the Middle Ages and he was an all-powerful knight, sitting atop a mighty horse, covered in armor and pointing at people with his fine-tipped sword. "Go fetch me water, you peasant!" he'd say, in his imaginings. But there were no peasants here, so he was stuck with names like dumbo. It would work better if the kid had big ears, but it still worked.

"You can run, but you can't hide!" yelled Chet. It wasn't very original, but it was all he could come up with on short notice.

There was another rustle. But no boy.

Chet turned the other way and thought he heard something again, but this time from the opposite direction. So he pivoted full circle. That's when he saw her.

Valencia Somerset.

Chet dropped the branch and moved closer to the tree. He told himself that he wanted to spy on her, but really he was hiding. The way she had glared at him at the Super Saver gave him the creeps.

And now here she was in the woods, holding something. A bowl.

She hadn't seen him. That was clear. She was focused on something else. Her eyes were narrow with concentration, like she was picking apart each leaf. She walked slowly, carefully, like she didn't want to disturb anything. And all the while she held the bowl with both hands.

It was obvious she was looking for an animal.

Or maybe not an animal. Maybe a creature.

Chet moved farther behind the tree so she wouldn't see him.

What if she was out here doing some kind of ritual sacrifice?

He remembered the blazing, angry look in her eyes. Something wasn't right in that girl's head, and it wasn't just her ears.

She crouched, peered through the trees, then stood and peered some more. What was in the bowl?

Maybe it was a human finger. Or one dozen chicken feet. Perhaps she'd cut the ears off rabbits and she wanted to feed them to some secret Bigfoot-like beast that lived in the forest.

She was evil, clearly. There was something strange about a girl who couldn't hear.

Unless she really *was* lying about it.

Chet mustered up the courage to make a noise that sounded like it could be an animal. He clucked his tongue. He hooted like an owl. Quietly at first, then louder. Valencia didn't react. He hooted again, louder still, but she just kept walking deliberately, with her bowl.

A few logical explanations crossed Chet's mind. Maybe she was taking care of stray cats. Only he hadn't seen a single one out here. There were only squirrels. And who would bring a bowl into the woods to feed squirrels? Clearly she was up to no good.

# 19
## Valencia

I don't just walk through the woods. I feel them. When the leaves shake in the wind, they tickle my skin. When I step on fallen branches, the snaps move through my feet. I can't see Sacred, but I know he's here and he isn't far. Where is he? To my left? To my right? I shake the bowl, and even though I can't hear the cereal pinging around, I can feel it. I know this will bring Sacred out of his hiding place.

"Sacred?" I call. "Sacred?"

I wonder if I should invent a sign name for Sacred. Dogs can learn sign language, easy. They can probably learn faster than people. I think I read that somewhere.

I've been trying to learn sign language, because I read that there are deaf people who know two languages—spoken English and American Sign Language—and I want to learn both. But it's tough when you don't have a teacher. I tried learning online, but it's hard to make any real sentences except "How are you?" and "What's your name?" I asked my parents once if I could take a class, but they don't think it's necessary because of my hearing aids. But the hearing aids don't work by themselves. I have to be able to see people's faces so I can put the sounds and lip movements together. Like two pieces in a puzzle. People always say, "Oh, I know," when I remind them to face me and talk slowly, but they still forget. Even my parents. They don't mean to, but they do.

I'm the only one who doesn't forget, because

I'm the only one solving the puzzle.

I call for Sacred again, and I wait.

It takes a while, but Sacred finally comes out of the trees. He's happy to see me like always. He picks up his pace and trots over like a horse. His black tail swings back and forth. When I put the bowl on the ground, he nudges my hand before digging in. His nose is cold.

It doesn't take him long to eat everything in the bowl. When he's done, I squat down and scratch behind his ears. My fingertips run along his fur. It's coarse and damp, like he's been rolling around in wet grass. Maybe he has. Who knows what Sacred does when I'm not around?

One thing I know for sure is I could never be a dog. They eat anything. Not me. I'm a picky eater. I don't like avocados, peaches, green beans, or peas. I like corn, but only if it's alone, sprinkled with salt and doused in butter. I like hamburgers, but not cheeseburgers. I like pizza, but only if it's plain. I like clementines, but not oranges. They look almost the same, but they're different. Clementines are much sweeter. Oranges just taste like oranges.

"Good boy," I say.

Sacred doesn't just take off and leave me when he's done eating. My friendship with Sacred has a lot to do with the fact that I bring him food, but it's not the only reason he likes me. I know this because he usually hangs around after he eats. He follows me, like an assistant. When I walk, he walks. When I sit down, he sits down. And when it's time for me to leave, he always knows somehow and goes back into the woods so he can keep rolling around in the grass or whatever he does when he's alone.

So Sacred and I walk across the clearing and I tell him what's been going on in my life.

"School is out for the summer," I say. "Everyone practically sprinted out of the building on the last day. I should be more excited, too, but I'm not. I'm not saying I *like* school—I mean, it's okay—but at least it's something to do. The good news is, I'll be able to come out here and check on you more often. I wish you could come home with me, or just any nice home, but this will be the next best thing."

We reach a fallen log that's between two trees. It's one of my favorite places to sit, and that's exactly what I do when I get there. I sit on the log, and Sacred sits at my feet.

"These people came by the house with pamphlets for their church," I continue. "And later I'm going to meet a fortune-teller named Kaori Tanaka."

Now that Sacred's all caught up, I take my zoological diary out of my bag, along with my pencil. I'm here to document the squirrels. They're my focus for the day. I like to pretend I'm Jane Goodall, except with squirrels instead of chimpanzees. It would be nice if there were chimpanzees in these woods, but that seems highly unlikely. Actually I'm not even sure there are chimpanzees anywhere in the United States, except for zoos. I'll have to research that later. I write in my diary: *where do chimps live?* And I put a star next to it. Any time I put a star next to something, it means "research later." I have a whole system going. You have to stay organized if you're going to study wildlife. Otherwise your notes will become a complete disaster.

I hate to admit it, but I started my first zoological diary because of Roberta. We used to be good friends, a long time before she gave me that *Famous Deaf People in History* book. The only reason she even came to the party was because her mother made her. I could tell. It was the same with most of the other girls, too. But before that we were BFFs, even though she got on my nerves a lot. Back then Roberta liked exploring the woods. She doesn't anymore—now she wears mascara, lip gloss, and sundresses—but back then, she liked to pretend that we were adventurers.

The only thing she was afraid of was snakes. Her dad had mentioned once that there were snakes in the woods, and from then on Roberta was terrified. To make her feel better, I learned everything I could about snakes. That way we'd know what to do to avoid getting bitten. I wrote it all down in a notebook. Here's what I found out:

1. NeVeR AntagoNIze A snaKe. DON'T poke it with sticks oR kick it oR AnythiNg like tHat, Unless you WANt it to Bite you,

2. NEVeR, NeVeR, NEVeR pick up a Snake by its tail.

3. STAy out oF TALL gRASS.

4. If you see oNe, ignoRe it aNd walk away quietly. Most people get Bitten when they TRy to get A closeR look, oR CaptuRe it.

5. If you get Bitten and the snake is poisonous, seek medical attention IMMediATeLy.

I shared all this information with Roberta, and she felt better. Life is a lot easier when you're prepared for stuff.

I wish I had been prepared when Roberta and I stopped being friends.

You know how sometimes you're friends with someone and they start hanging out with other people and eventually you're not friends anymore, but you can't remember when it all happened? Well, that's not how it was with Roberta. I know the exact date: October twelfth, fourth grade. Roberta and the other girls were playing chase and I was doing my best to play, too. But after the game was over, she walked up to me and said, "We don't want you to play with us anymore."

"Why?" I asked, even though I already knew the answer.

"The how-tos are too hard," she said. "And you're too slow."

The how-tos were what we called the three

ways to talk so I could understand: face me, don't cover your mouth, and speak clearly.

When she said I was too slow, I knew what that meant, too.

When we raced, I could never tell exactly when Megan Lewis called out, "Ready, set, go!" I could see she was getting ready to call it out, but I was never totally sure she had said all three words. When we played musical chairs, I couldn't tell when the music stopped. With hide-and-seek, I never knew when ready-or-not-here-I-come happened. I always figured it out, but I was usually two or three steps behind everyone else. It slowed down the game. I knew that. I guess I just didn't know that everyone else knew it, too. I thought I'd fooled them. But Roberta set me straight.

"Maybe you can find new friends," she said.

Like I could snap my fingers and there they'd be.

That night, I cried on my mom's lap. That's how upset I was. And my mom said that if they were real friends, they would have figured out a game that all of us could play. I can't stand when she says stuff like that. It makes me think she doesn't get it. Bad friends were better than no friends. And besides, I thought they were my real friends in the first place. That was the whole reason I was crying.

But I'm solo now, and everything's working out great.

I know I prayed to Saint Rene for a friend to protect me from Kaori Tanaka—just in case—but I'm over it. I'm doing just fine. Here I am, sketching in my journal, looking out for squirrels, with a loyal dog at my feet. He doesn't care if I can't hear him, and he doesn't need any how-tos.

What more could I ask for?

# 20
## The Question of Yelling

Virgil could not recall a single time in his life when he had yelled. He was sure he must have. Who goes eleven years of their life without yelling once? But he had an excellent memory, and he couldn't remember yelling. He wondered if he had even yelled when he was a baby. He would have to ask his mother. She would know.

"You're the quietest boy in the history of the whole Salinas family," his mother used to say. And then, "If we ever take you back home, we'll have to teach you how to speak. Otherwise no one will ever see you and you might get squashed by a carabao or a jeepney." This made her laugh, even though she'd said it a million times already, so Virgil wasn't sure how she could still think it was funny. He hadn't found it very funny the first time, to tell you the truth. When he imagined himself getting squashed by a carabao or a jeepney, it terrified him, even though he wasn't completely sure what either of those things were.

It's not that he felt unloved, exactly. He just didn't know why his parents were so preoccupied with him "coming out of his shell." What was so bad about a shell, anyway? Turtles had survived on earth more than two hundred million years— longer than snakes or crocodiles, even. And turtles lived a long time, too. American box turtles lived to be over a hundred, and they had excellent eyesight and senses of smell. Turtles truly were extraordinary animals. What if people had forced turtles to come out of their shells two hundred million years ago? They probably wouldn't exist anymore.

Virgil leaned against the musty wall of the well. There was a short ledge that circled the bottom, but it didn't give him enough of a boost to reach the ladder. He wondered if he should sit. Was sitting down the same as giving up?

He wondered what time it was.

He wondered if he should yell.

It seemed like the sensible thing to do, but when he opened his mouth, he imagined his cries for help sailing up, up, up, booming across the woods, shaking the leaves, frightening the birds, and landing on the thick, waxy ears of Chet Bullens. Then he imagined the Bull charging forward, grunting and panting and sniffing him out like a wolf. And then he saw the Bull pick up the cover of the well and shut him inside forever.

*Best to wait awhile,* Virgil thought, until the Bull had most likely gone home.

Trouble was, he had no idea how long "awhile" was because he didn't have a watch and his cell phone was broken. So he decided to go by feel. Did it feel like ten minutes or forty since he'd been down below? Who could say? Virgil wasn't great with numbers in the first place, and he certainly wasn't great at telling time, with or without a clock. It was something that had once frustrated his dad so much that he'd thrown up his hands one afternoon and said, *"Ay dios ko!* Never mind, Virgilio, just figure out the beginnings and ends and don't worry about the time in the middle."

Virgil wasn't sure if this was a beginning, an end, the middle, or what. All he knew was that his legs ached and the sun didn't seem as bright, so he threw back his head and called out, "Hello! Hello!" It didn't feel like much noise, though. Could anyone hear him? He needed to be louder.

"Hello! Hello!"

Gulliver's whiskers stopped moving. His round black eyes fixed on Virgil from his nest in the backpack, which Virgil was wearing backward so he could lean against the wall and watch Gulliver at the same time.

"Hello! Hello! Help! Help!"

He'd never called out for help before. It sounded strange. But if he was ever in need of help, this was it. He mustered all the strength he could—from deep, deep down—and took a large breath that filled his chest like a balloon.

Then he yelled, his most powerful yet. "Help! *Help!*"

His voice startled him. It didn't sound like his. It charged through his body. Down to his toes. Who knew he could be this loud?

If only his parents could hear him now.

# 21
## Valencia

Squirrels are very busy creatures. They must be the busiest animals in the world. They're so busy that they're forgetful. I once read that squirrels spend most of their time hiding acorns for later, but then they forget where they hid them. That's where new trees come from. There must be thousands of acorns buried in the ground here. Maybe even millions. If I ever wind up as the only person on the face of the earth like in my nightmare and I don't have electricity or fresh vegetables, I'll dig into the ground and find all the forgotten acorns. Then I could feed myself for months, maybe years. And when I locate civilization again, people will ask, "How did you survive, Valencia?" And I will say, "I ate all the acorns the squirrels left behind." And people will think, *Wow, she is really clever.*

From my observations I've learned that squirrels keep nests in the trees. At first I thought they lived in the ground, but now I know better. They use twigs and leaves to build nests in the branches. They look like birds' nests at first glance. I wish I could climb one of the trees and get a good look, but that would be hard. I'd probably wind up falling forty feet and breaking twenty-seven bones or something. Plus, I don't want to interfere with nature.

Sometimes I do interfere, though. Only when it's necessary. For example, a few minutes ago I gathered a handful of acorns and placed them at the base of the pine tree near my fallen log. I wanted to see what the squirrels would do with them, and guess what? Within minutes one of them scurried down, took a few of them, and darted off. They must have some kind of nut radar.

Squirrels are part of the rodent family. I wonder if all rodents like nuts? I've never seen a rat with an acorn, but then again you don't usually stumble on rats in nature. I wonder why?

I write in my diary.

☆ Do OTHeR RodeNTS
    liKe Nuts?
☆ How coMe I NeVeR See
    RATs in the Woods?

It's almost time to meet Kaori. I'd be lying if I said I wasn't nervous. I stand up, put my diary in my bag, and close my eyes.

"Dear Saint Rene," I say. "I'm about to go see Kaori Tanaka. I have two favors to ask. First, please watch over me, just in case. Second, please help her help me get rid of my nightmare so I can have a good summer. Or at least a summer with good nights' sleep."

I open my eyes, take a deep breath, and start walking to the other side of the woods. I'm so lost in thought that I almost don't notice the old well, and I always notice it, because it's one of my favorite things. I think it's from colonial times, but I'm not sure. It's still in decent shape. Probably because it's made of stone—all except the heavy board that covers it. But something looks different now.

The board has been moved.

I walk up to the well. Sure enough, the mouth is wide open. Someone's been goofing off. And here's evidence: a small pile of rocks, neatly placed. I bet someone opened the well so they could throw them inside. Seems like a boring way to pass an afternoon, but I try it anyway. I drop them in, one by one.

It's dark down there.

Very dark.

It makes me think of the Crystal Caverns, only something's not right. I don't know what it is, but I shudder and snatch my hands away.

Did I hear something? Or was it my imagination?

I take a small step back like something might jump out at me, then lean forward and peer in again. Blackness. Sometimes when I can't hear something, I feel it. Am I feeling something now?

I should put the lid back. That's what's bothering me. An animal might fall inside. What if a squirrel went exploring and couldn't get out?

Saint Rene blessed the children so he could protect them. That's how I like to think of myself, with the squirrels. I'm not saying I'm as brave as Saint Rene—I mean, he got kidnapped and everything—only that I'd like to be like him. I know the squirrels can take care of themselves, mostly. But the open well might confuse them.

*Yes, I better put it back.*

So I do.

But even when the well is safely covered, I have a weird feeling. It doesn't go away—not even when I'm out of the woods and crossing the street to Kaori's house.

# 22
## Imagine You Are Someplace Else

The darkness had teeth that snapped and clenched, and here was Virgil, sitting at the bottom of its throat. He couldn't even see his hand in front of his face. There wasn't a sliver of light anywhere. Not a single pinprick.

"The Bull wants to kill me," he said.

He never would have believed it, not truly—but what other explanation could there be? His cries for help had traveled through the trees and landed on the Bull's waxy ears, just like he'd predicted. Virgil had shielded Gulliver when the stones fell. Then the light went away. The Bull wanted to taunt them, then kill him. It was the only logical explanation. Who else would do such a thing?

Now his heart beat quickly. Too quickly. *Maybe I'm having a heart attack,* he thought. Was this what they felt like? Could eleven-year-olds have heart attacks?

He couldn't breathe, either. His lungs had been stolen by the darkness. He sputtered and clutched his backpack close to him, both arms wrapped around it like a life raft. Gulliver chirped, not knowing any better. Or maybe he did, and he was saying good-bye.

When Gulliver stopped chirping, a strange sound filled the well—a wail mixed with a gasp and a hiccup. Virgil frantically searched the darkness before he realized the sound was coming from him. So maybe he wasn't going to die of a heart attack. It would be a breathing attack instead. Or both.

Virgil's breath caught in his throat. Now he was half gasping, half choking.

"Calm down, calm down," he said to himself, only because of the gasping it sounded more like "Ca-AH-lm-AH-AH-D-D-AH-OWN." But it worked, kind of. He stopped half choking, anyway. But he didn't let go of the backpack. He told himself he was protecting Gulliver, but he knew it was the other way around.

The bottom of a well is a quiet, quiet place. Virgil had never realized how noisy the world was until there was nothing to hear. No distant cars driving by. No humming of a nearby air conditioner. No birds chirping. He couldn't even hear the turning of a leaf.

"This is the end," he said. He perched on the low ledge. "No one will know where I am. Generations of Salinases will continue on forever, far into the future, and not one of them will ever know that I'm here."

People would say, "We once had a boy called Virgilio in our family, but no one knows what became of him," and they would make the sign of the cross. All the while, his bones would lie at the bottom of the pit, with Gulliver's little bones next to him, so small that they'd look like thread.

Virgil's throat was dry. His head suddenly felt very heavy, like someone had placed a brick on his forehead and asked him to balance it there. He opened his mouth to take a deep, deep breath, but he couldn't. His lungs felt full of air and empty all at once. His body was a bundle of nerves, all being pulled and snapped at the same time.

And now it wasn't just the darkness or the silence. It was the smell, too. Mildew and old, stale water. It reminded him of how the sink in the kitchen smelled when the drain clogged up.

He closed his eyes. *"Imagine you are someplace else."* That's what his mother used to tell him when he was very little and had bad dreams. Before she called him Turtle. Before they figured out that he wouldn't be perfect like his brothers. *"Imagine you are someplace else."*

He imagined his bedroom, with Gulliver rattling the water bottle. He imagined Kaori's house, with the circle rug and the incense that smelled like burned flowers. He imagined Lola at the table, reading her newspaper and shaking her head.

All the imagining might have worked if Virgil's ears had been closed instead of his eyes, but because they were open and alert, they picked up a distant sound in the darkness.

*Ignore it,* thought Virgil. *Probably just Gulliver.*

Only he knew what Gulliver sounded like, and this wasn't it. Gulliver's noises were harmless and simple—squeaks when he was hungry, chirps when he was happy. Guinea pigs didn't do much else. They certainly didn't ruffle anything. They didn't have anything to ruffle.

And that's what this sound was.

*"Imagine you are someplace else. Imagine you are someplace else."*

He went back to his bedroom, but it faded as soon as he thought of it. Kaori's circle rug vanished, too. Even Lola and her table were swallowed up.

The sound—what was it?

Wings, that's what. Wings being opened. Wings being tucked.

A colony of bats, maybe, ready to descend with their daggered mouths.

Louder, now.

Virgil didn't dare open his eyes. His feet were blocks of cement, his legs were rubber bands, and his mouth was clenched so tightly that he was breathing only through his nose—but it wasn't breathing, really. More like hyperventilating.

The sound of quick, useless breaths spurting

through his nostrils filled the space, but the rustling grew even louder, and he realized now that it couldn't be bats.

This was something fuller.

This had plumes.

Feathers.

Wings that could blanket an entire village.

This was Pah.

# 23
## The Issue of Time

Kaori Tanaka's first word was "nomad," even though she had no nomadic blood. Not as far as she could tell, judging by her parents. But one thing she did inherit from her parents—specifically, her mother—was a keen sense of time. One of her first orders of business as the older sister was to teach Gen how to tell time. Unfortunately, Gen didn't have much of a knack for it.

"What time is it?" Kaori had asked one

afternoon a few years before, when Gen was just starting to learn. Kaori had drawn a clock on a sheet of paper. Anyone could see it was three thirty—the peak of the witching hour—but Gen stared at the clock blankly. Instead of giving the right time, Gen sat down with her legs stretched in front of her and grabbed her toes. She'd always been a wiggly girl.

"I don't know," Gen had said. "But who cares? All I have to do is look at Mom's cell phone or the microwave, and it will tell me right away, with the numbers."

"This has numbers, too," Kaori said.

"But it doesn't tell me straight out."

Kaori sighed. "Life can't always be straight out, you know."

That was the first and last time Kaori had tried to teach Gen how to tell time, but she never stopped hounding her about one of life's most important lessons: be punctual.

One of the things Kaori appreciated most about Virgil was his punctuality. If he said he would be somewhere at eight thirteen and forty seconds, that's what time he would arrive. Sometimes a little earlier, but never later. Not even by a minute.

That's why she knew something was wrong even before she looked at the clock and saw that he was fifteen minutes late.

"It's not like him to just not show up. He didn't even give us a 'Sorry, can't make it,'" Kaori told Gen. They were standing side by side at the living-room window, looking through the blinds, waiting for Virgil's skinny little body to come up the walk. "It doesn't seem right that he wouldn't text, especially because he knows how precious my time is. And I have that new client coming later."

"Maybe he forgot," said Gen.

"Doubtful," said Kaori.

"Maybe his mom or dad made him do something else and he didn't have a chance to tell us."

That seemed more likely. Parents had a way of getting in the middle of things and screwing everything up. But still. . . .

"It doesn't seem right," said Kaori. "He still would have texted or something." She opened the front door and took a step outside. She crossed her arms and scanned the road with her dark, lined eyes. This proved the level of her concern. Kaori never stepped outside for clients. She always demanded the password. When you have powers of second sight, you have to protect yourself. Look what happened to the Salem witches.

Gen stood next to her and crossed her arms, too. If their parents had been home, they would have told them to shut the door because they were letting all the air conditioning out and didn't they know how much money they were wasting? But praise be to the ancestors, Mr. and Mrs. Tanaka had Saturday errands.

"I have a bad feeling," Kaori said. She tipped

her head back and looked to the sky for signs. But it was a bright blue, cloudless day. Some would say it was a beautiful day, but Kaori thought rainstorms had much more personality.

Gen's eyes widened. "Maybe you should consult the crystals."

Oh, yes. The crystals. How could she have forgotten the crystals? But those were reserved for special occasions. She wasn't sure if a client being twenty minutes late qualified.

"Let's text him again, just for good measure," Kaori said.

They walked back inside and went to Kaori's bedroom, where she had laid her cell phone just outside the door. She preferred not to use her phone in the chamber because she wasn't sure how the world of the hereafter felt about such things. She'd explained cell phones and the internet to the spirits, so they were all up to speed, but you never know.

Virgil didn't answer the text, so Kaori called. It went straight to his generic voicemail. Kaori hung up, leaned against the wall in the hallway, and chewed her bottom lip.

At eleven thirty she developed a pit of concern in her belly.

At eleven thirty-five, she considered that something could be gravely wrong.

By eleven forty, she was convinced that Virgil Salinas had met a terrible fate and it was time to consult the crystals.

She kept them in a small velvet sling bag inside a locked box behind a stack of spell books under her bed. Gen was the only one who knew where the crystals were, and it was her greatest secret as far as both of them were concerned. Gen had to swear on her past, present, and future lives that she would never reveal the location of the crystals for as long as she lived.

When she asked Kaori where the crystals came

from, Kaori put her finger to her lips and said, "The keeper of secrets may ask no questions."

In truth, Kaori had gotten them at a garage sale. Mrs. Tanaka loved going to garage sales. She thought it was "absolutely wonderful" that Kaori wanted to go along because she called it "mother-daughter time," but really Kaori just wanted to see what kind of treasures people were giving away for a nickel. That's where she had found the crystals.

The woman selling them said you were supposed to use them to fill flower vases. "For decoration," the lady said. But Kaori knew better. The secrets of the universe buried themselves in unusual and beautiful objects such as these, and only a select few could pull those secrets out. So she had bought the crystals for ten cents.

Kaori locked her bedroom door as Gen wiggled under the bed for the box. Once she had it, she carried it gingerly to the rug. Kaori opened it, removed the bag, and shook out the crystals. Then

 170

they both leaned forward. A close inspection.

"What do you see?" asked Gen quietly.

Kaori studied each crystal without touching it. They were all different colors. Red, blue, clear, and pink. She scanned the clear plastic one with particular interest.

"He didn't forget the appointment," she said. "He's been detained somehow."

"Detayed? What's that mean?"

"Not detayed. *Detained*. Held up."

Gen gasped. "You mean with a gun?"

"No, no. Not held up with a gun. Just . . . interrupted somehow." She straightened her back and added, with some authority, "Something has prevented him from being here."

"But we know that already. Since he's not here."

Kaori ignored her. Gen was a helpful assistant but could be insufferable.

"Something's happened," said Kaori. "Of this, I am certain."

# 24
## Valencia

I've never been to a psychic's house before, but I guess I expected something different, like a big glowing sign that said PALM READING or FORTUNES HERE. But instead the address led me to a regular house. I'm not sure what to think of this. Is this a good sign or a bad sign? Does this mean Kaori is or is not a crazy person?

There's only one way to find out.

I walk up and ring the doorbell. I can tell that

it works by the way it vibrates under my fingertip. You'd be surprised how many people have broken doorbells. I stare at the door with my heart beating, but I don't have to wait long before it opens, and a little girl is standing there. She looks like she's in first grade or something. She has a pink jump rope slung over her shoulder. She's a lot younger than I thought, but at least she's not a serial killer. No wonder I couldn't find her online anywhere. She's probably too young to even use the computer.

"Password?" she says.

"Venus rises in the west."

The girl eyes my hearing aids. "What're those?"

"Hearing aids," I say.

I wait for her reaction.

Sometimes people get scared when they find out you can't hear. They don't want to talk to you, or they don't know where to look. Their eyes dart all around like they're searching for an invisible portal to take them somewhere else.

But this girl just says, "You talk funny."

I say, "I know. It's because I'm deaf."

"Oh," she says, and opens the door wide.

The house is very neat and clean, and it smells like incense. Curls of smoke drift out of a room down the hall. This is where the girl leads me.

*Dear Saint Rene, if there's a crazy psycho killer in that smoky room, please protect me. Amen.*

Turns out, there's no crazy psycho killer, just another girl, about my age. I know right away this is Kaori. She's standing in front of a huge star chart with her hands on her hips. She turns when I walk in. Her face looks distracted. Her eyebrows are doing this slight wrinkle in the middle, which is what happens when you're worried. You know how I said you can tell a lot about a person by their eyes? Well, eyebrows have even more to say.

"Are you Just Renee?" she asks.

At first I'm confused, but then I remember that I gave her a fake, just-in-case name.

"Yes."

The little girl walks up to her sister so they're both facing me.

"She has hearing aids and she talks funny," the little girl says.

I tell them about the how-tos and expect them to look nervous or uncomfortable, but neither of them does. Kaori seems to have other things on her mind.

"I'm Kaori," she says. "I apologize for being a little distracted. I have a client who was supposed to be here two hours ago, and I'm worried. You didn't see him, did you?"

"What's he look like?"

"He's small, kinda scrawny, with brown skin and dark hair," Kaori says. She looks right at me and talks slowly, just like I asked. "He looks scared all the time, and he carries a purple backpack. He's eleven."

"His name is Virgil," the little girl adds. "My name is Gen."

"Small, scrawny, with dark hair?"

Gen and Kaori nod.

I know I didn't see any boy like that this morning, but something about the description feels familiar.

"And a purple backpack," Gen says. "And looks scared all the time."

I feel like I know this person.

The name Virgil doesn't mean anything to me, but that's because it's hard for me to remember names. I'm much better with faces.

I didn't see anyone on my way to Kaori's, though. That's for sure.

"I haven't seen him," I say.

She frowns. "I'm sure he'll turn up." After a moment she forces a smile and says, "Let's talk about your dreams. Are they good or bad?"

"If they were good, I wouldn't be here," I say.

"Excellent point," Kaori says. She points to a circle rug and tells me to sit down. I do.

"Now," she says, sitting across from me, next to Gen. "Let us begin."

I can't help but notice that her worried look hasn't disappeared.

Not completely.

# 25
## The Girl Who Didn't Know Her Destiny

Virgil covered his ears. He pressed his palms against them until it hurt. His heartbeat moved from his chest to his head, and yet the rustling was still there. Louder somehow. The sound of ruffled feathers managed to soar above everything—the *THA-thump-THA-thump-THA-thump*ing of his heart and the *huff-huff-huff* through his nostrils—but he refused to open his eyes. He couldn't anyway, because they were glued shut. His eyeballs ached.

The apples of his cheeks, too. His whole face had been balled into a knot and tightened.

No, he couldn't look. He wouldn't.

The wings moved again. Were they closer? They felt closer.

Was that a feather on his cheek, or—?

He flinched, the same way he did when teachers called on him even though he hadn't raised his hand. "Can you tell us the answer, Virgil?" they'd ask, looking right at him.

He shook his head. No, no, no.

"What is the solution—does anyone know? Virgil?"

One time, in Ms. Murray's class, he had said— in a low, low voice—exactly what he was thinking. "But I didn't raise my hand."

"Sometimes life calls on you even when you don't raise your hand," she'd said.

The wings were bigger now, he could tell. They were spreading, tips touching opposite sides of the well, taking up all the space that he and Gulliver couldn't manage to fill.

Pah.

When would he feel the talons?

"Open your eyes," a voice said. "That's the solution."

The voice wasn't his. It was coming from inside the well, through his hands and heart and failed breaths. It was embodied, as if from beyond. It was a girl's voice, one he'd never heard before.

Virgil opened his mouth—dry like parched grass—to say, "Who said that?" But he wasn't sure he'd actually said anything until she replied.

"Me."

The voice breezed through the well like steam drifting from a cup of hot chocolate.

Virgil pushed himself back against the wall as far as he could.

"I don't want to open my eyes," he said. This time he was sure he'd spoken aloud.

"The more scared you are, the bigger Pah gets," the girl said. "Besides, he's not as bad as you think. Most things aren't."

She sounded so calm that Virgil almost believed her. She reminded him of Lola, even though she was just a girl. But where had she come from? He wasn't certain of much, especially not now—but he knew there hadn't been a girl in the well when he climbed down.

"I don't believe in ghosts," he said, even though that wasn't true at all.

"Me neither," the girl replied.

He realized now that his breathing had calmed and he couldn't hear Pah anymore, but he still didn't want to open his eyes. What if Pah was staring back at him, widening his enormous beak?

"He won't be," said the girl. "Trust me."

How did she know what he was thinking?

"I hear by seeing," she replied.

Virgil unscrewed his face. His hands were

making his ears sweat, but he didn't dare uncover them. He opened his eyes instead. Slowly. Slowly.

Darkness.

More darkness.

But no pointed beak. No feathers. No talons.

No Pah.

The well was just as it had been.

His heartbeat slowed—still racing and ready for takeoff, but no longer desperate to crash through his chest.

"See?" the girl said proudly.

He moved his hands to his sides—slowly, slowly—and darted his eyes around in the dark.

"Where are you?" he asked. It came out as a whisper.

"I'm all around. Can't you tell?"

Yes, he could tell. Her voice came from everywhere, like the well itself was speaking.

"Wells can't talk," said Virgil.

He placed his palm on one of the stones

without moving any other part of his body.

It felt like the well was *breathing*.

"I can see that you're afraid, Bayani, but you needn't be."

"How? How can you see?"

"I see by listening."

"My name isn't Bayani."

"It is to me," the girl said.

"Who are you?"

"Ruby San Salvador."

The name sounded vaguely familiar.

"The girl who didn't know her destiny," she explained. "Remember?"

Yes, he remembered. From Lola's story.

"What are you doing here?" Virgil's voice was small.

Pah had disappeared.

For now.

"Fulfilling my destiny," said Ruby.

"Your destiny is to live in a well?"

"No. My destiny is to help people in trouble."

Virgil clutched his backpack.

"Can you move the cover and help me up the ladder?"

"Of course not. You need arms to move things."

"Oh," said Virgil.

Silence filled the well.

Gulliver squeaked.

"I guess it's hopeless," whispered Virgil.

"Oh, Bayani," Ruby replied. "Nothing is ever hopeless."

# 26
## Interpretation of a Dream

It was true that Kaori had studied dreams. Well, on the internet, at least. She believed the unconscious was a powerful force. Quite powerful indeed. And sometimes the brain needed dreams to get rid of all the things that made people afraid or anxious. To Kaori, the solution was clear: overcome your fears, and the nightmares go away.

After hearing the details of Just Renee's

nightmare, she knew exactly what the problem was. It was clear as anything.

When she was sure Just Renee was looking at her, she said, "You're afraid of girls in blue dresses."

Renee tilted her head skeptically, then shook it. They were sitting on the zodiac rug. The usual placements—Kaori and Gen on one side, client on the other.

"I don't think that's it," offered Gen.

Kaori turned toward her sister. "Excuse me, but you're not the expert here. And besides, how do you know my interpretation isn't accurate?"

Gen shrugged. "Just seems too . . . I don't know . . . too *obvious*."

"Sometimes the simple answer is the real answer," Kaori said. She turned back to Renee, who looked unconvinced. "But I'll concentrate further, just in case I may be wrong."

She stressed the *may* part.

She closed her eyes and pictured Renee standing in that field all by herself.

"You're scared," said Kaori. "You're afraid of being alone."

When she opened her eyes, Renee's face was knotted like she'd just eaten something sour.

"I'm not *scared*," she said, like it was a bitter word she needed to spit out. "I *like* being alone. It's easier that way."

Kaori and Gen exchanged looks. Kaori wasn't used to being challenged by her clients. Then again, her only other client was Virgil.

"Well," said Kaori. She spoke carefully, pausing here and there to make sure Renee was getting all her important information. "I could be wrong. But it seems to me that you feel alone, or maybe you're afraid of feeling alone. That's why you get scared when you look around and everyone's gone. Because it's like you live in a bubble. Everyone looks at you like you're invisible. And then one day . . . you *are* invisible. That would be scary to anyone."

Gen nodded with vigor.

Just Renee made a face that was a cross between a frown and a scowl.

"I *like* being alone," she insisted. She crossed her arms.

"Oh," Kaori said.

"Alone is good. It's less trouble."

"Maybe I'm way off. Probably because I'm worried about Virgil. I can't seem to concentrate."

Gen nodded again. "It's true," she said. "She stared at those lines for a really long time before you got here." She pointed to the star chart.

Renee glanced at the chart, then looked back at the sisters. Kaori wanted to explain that they weren't merely lines, but she figured it was best to leave well enough alone, as her father liked to say.

"Well," Renee said. She uncrossed her arms. "I can help you look for him. If you want."

Kaori eyed her new client curiously. Renee was stubborn, but with a quick-fizzling temper. Interesting. She wondered what sign she was. Leo? Aries?

"Hey, what sign are you?" Kaori asked.

But Renee was busy standing up, so she didn't realize Kaori was talking to her.

# 27
## Valencia

Okay, so maybe being alone isn't always the best. It would be nice if I could go back to the days when I was part of a group. I mean, it's good to have the same people to sit with at lunch every day instead of just sitting wherever. And sure, it'd be good to have some plans over the summer besides feeding Sacred or watching squirrels and birds' nests. But it's not like I'm *afraid* or anything.

Kaori says we should eat before we start our

search-party strategy, so the three of us go into the kitchen. I realize I'm hungrier than I thought. It's way past lunchtime already.

Kaori pulls out a loaf of bread and some cold cuts to make sandwiches. I make a ham sandwich with mustard and nothing else. Gen makes bologna with about five pounds of mayo. Kaori has ham, lettuce, and tomato and cuts off all the crust.

As we all munch on our sandwiches in the Tanakas' kitchen—which is big and clean and smells like potatoes, with a nice table topped with tall, skinny candles—Kaori says that we need to start with the obvious places first.

"The only obvious place is his house," she says, her mouth half full. "We need to go over there and see if he's home."

"That sounds easy enough," I say. I only used two slices of thin ham for my sandwich since I thought it was the polite thing to do, but now I wish I'd thrown on an extra. I taste mostly mustard and bread. But a sandwich is a sandwich when you're hungry.

"Not as easy as you would think," Kaori continues. She pauses. "You're the one who has to go to the door and ask for him."

I swallow. "Me? Why me? I don't even know him."

She takes a swig of her drink and wipes her mouth with her sleeve while talking at the same time, so I miss the first part of her sentence. I catch the tail end: ". . . he might get in trouble."

Now I get it. If Virgil's parents think he's with Kaori and she shows up looking for him, he could get in trouble, especially if he's off doing something he's not supposed to be doing.

"Where does he live?" I ask.

Kaori motions in a random direction. "In a nice house on the other side of the woods. He goes to Boyd Middle."

"So do I," I say. "I'm going into seventh."

"So is Virgil!" Gen exclaims, a gob of mayo on her bottom lip.

"Are you sure you don't know him?" asks Kaori.

"I don't know," I say. "I'm not good with names." I motion toward my hearing aids to explain why. "Just faces."

It's hard for me to make out what Gen says next because her mouth is full of food, but I gather that she's telling me what Virgil's face looks like.

Brown.

Skinny.

Sad.

I wonder how Gen would describe my face to someone else.

I wouldn't want to be described as sad. But maybe I am.

Not right now, though.

Right now I'm just a girl eating a sandwich, waiting to see what happens next.

# 28
## Bali

Virgil tried once again to shove the toe of his sneaker between two of the heavy stones of the well, but they were so densely packed that he couldn't gain enough footing to step up and reach the ladder. He also tried the ledge again, but it wasn't tall enough. Neither was he. He jumped just in case he'd suddenly sprouted ten inches, but his fingertips never brushed the bottom rung. He wasn't even sure where the ladder was, anyway. It was so dark.

He sat, exhausted, and fed Gulliver a dandelion.

"I wonder how long it will take for someone to start searching for me," Virgil said. He thought about the Stone Boy.

"How do you know someone hasn't started already?" said Ruby.

"I hope they show up before Pah comes back."

"Why don't you rest instead of worrying about Pah? He's not here now. That's what matters."

"I can't rest. It's too quiet," said Virgil.

"Silence is good sometimes," Ruby replied. "That's when you're able to hear best."

"Hear what?"

"Your *thoughts*, Bayani."

"That's just it. I don't want to have any thoughts, because then I'll have to think about how I'm trapped down here with no way out."

Ruby sighed. "That's the problem. People don't want to listen to their thoughts, so they fill the world with noise."

"I wouldn't mind the quiet if I were someplace else."

"Like where?"

Virgil brought his backpack closer. "Bali."

"What's Bali?"

"I don't know," said Virgil. "It's a place people always want to go." His parents talked about it often. They even had brochures.

"Why? What's it look like?"

"Magical, I think. Otherwise, why would so many people want to go there?"

Virgil imagined a bright purple sky with thick blue clouds. Any time it rained in Bali, the clouds cracked open and fat drops of laughing gas fell down on everyone. No one could stop laughing in Bali. They drank out of golden goblets and laughed and laughed. They didn't care if people were in their shells or not. And the sun shone all the time, so the whole place was bathed in light. Anything the light touched belonged to the sun gods and the sun gods never allowed any evil to pass through Bali's borders. There were soldiers stationed at every entrance just in case, but no one dared to even step close. The sun gods' only mortal enemies were the One Hundred Kings of Darkness. But the kings had been banished to the core of the earth, where they'd been asleep for five thousand years.

The One Hundred Kings of Darkness couldn't sleep forever. Everyone knew that. But no one knew when they'd wake up. So the sun gods appointed one special warrior to defeat them. The warrior spent years in training so he'd be prepared if the kings ever opened their eyes—all two hundred of them.

"It's you, Bayani!" said Ruby. "*You're* the sun god warrior."

"I'm no warrior," said Virgil. He leaned his head back against the stone and breathed in the mildew. He didn't notice it as much now. "My brothers, maybe. But not me."

*"Pshah!"*

"What do you mean, *pshah*? They're strong and everything."

"What's that got to do with anything?"

"Well, I'm just saying. They aren't scrawny and weak like me."

"Weakness has nothing to do with how much you weigh." Ruby hesitated. "Sure, maybe they can play sports and lift things, but that doesn't mean they're strong. There are many different ways to be strong. And being a warrior has nothing to do with size. Surely there have been small warriors before."

Virgil thought of Paulito and the Jungle Dragon, which had been one of Lola's favorite stories before she switched to tales about crocodiles and rocks eating children. The story of Paulito had a much happier ending.

"Tell me about him," said Ruby.

"How do you know what I'm thinking?"

"I was listening."

"But I didn't say anything."

"What difference does that make?" Ruby said. "Tell me the story. I love stories."

Virgil didn't consider himself much of a storyteller, but he gathered all the pieces of Paulito together in his head and began the best way he knew how—at the beginning.

"Paulito was only one inch tall, but he wanted to be king. Not because he was greedy or anything like that, but because his village wouldn't stop arguing and fighting over petty nonsense." Virgil remembered Lola using that phrase specifically, "petty nonsense," because he had had to ask her what it meant.

"When your house is on fire and you straighten the pillows before you leave," Lola had said.

"Everyone laughed at him. They said a man who was one inch tall could never rule a village. They got so worked up that they started arguing again."

Gulliver chirped, so Virgil fed him a dandelion. He didn't feed him more than one at a time, though. Gulliver had to ration his food. Virgil wondered if he would have to eat dandelions, too. What would happen if he did? Would he die of dandelion poisoning? And what about water? How long could he go without water?

Virgil put his hand on his throat. Suddenly he was very thirsty.

"Then what happened, Bayani?" Ruby urged. "I hope that's not the end."

"Oh. Sorry." Virgil dropped his hand and scratched behind Gulliver's ears. "I'm not very good at telling stories. Not like Lola."

Thinking of Lola made Virgil sick and nauseous, like there were a million tears deep inside of him that wanted to come out. What would she be doing now? Folding the laundry? Ironing shirts? Pulling weeds from the garden? Fussing at his mother for buying too many bananas? Whatever it was, she probably wasn't thinking that one of her stories had finally come true—a well had eaten her grandson.

"Just try," Ruby said.

Virgil swallowed. "While they argued, he gathered grains of sand from the beach. He could only carry a handful at a time. The village was so busy arguing that they didn't notice what he was doing. Then big ships came and tried to invade. But they couldn't get in because Paulito had built a fortress, one handful at a time."

Ruby waited. "And?"

"And they crowned him king of the island. He was the best king they ever had."

Those one million pushed-down tears crept upward.

He missed his Lola.

"I'm no warrior. I'm no Paulito," he said. "Paulito wouldn't hide from the Bull. Paulito was brave. He wouldn't be scared."

"It's not being brave if you aren't scared."

"Yes, but I don't do anything. I don't fight at all."

"There are many ways to fight. Maybe you just haven't been ready. But you'll be ready next time."

"I don't want a next time."

"My dear Bayani," said Ruby. "There is always a next time."

*Bayani* meant hero. Virgil remembered now. He sat in the silence of the deep, dark well, suddenly remembering things. One thing he remembered was the day his parents and his math teacher told him he'd be going to the resource room every Thursday because of his multiplication tables.

Virgil's mind had wandered that day as he sat in the uncomfortable chair across from Mr. Linton with his parents on either side of him. Instead of listening to the details of what made him "special," he heard "multiplication tables" and began to imagine a never-ending assembly line of tables—

like the kind you get at Ikea—cloning themselves and stacking up, up, up. And he pictured himself standing near the bottom one, leaning back and trying to see the top of the Ikea mountain. Only he couldn't, because he was special.

Mr. Linton explained to Virgil and his parents that going to the resource room meant Virgil would get more individual attention. It didn't mean there was anything wrong with him, Mr. Linton hastened to add.

At the time, Virgil had thought, *That's not true. There is something wrong—I can't do my multiplication tables. There's a right way to do them, and there's a wrong way. And if I was doing them the right way, I wouldn't be here.*

But he kept his mouth shut.

He didn't mind going to the resource room, anyway. It's not like he was having a blast with Mr. Linton. So if he needed more individual time, that was fine with him. He was pretty sure no one would notice he was gone, anyhow.

Besides, it turned out to be the best day of Virgil's entire school year, because that's where he saw Valencia for the first time.

She was wearing a purple shirt. Her hair was in two perfect braids. The hems of her jeans were smudged with dirt, and she carried a journal under her arm that Virgil was desperate to read. Sometimes he'd wonder: if she accidentally left it behind on the desk, would he sneak a peek? Or would he be a good person and guard it so no one else could? He liked to think it was the second one. But he really longed to know what she wrote and sketched about. It made Virgil want his own journal. Maybe he had things to say and he just didn't know it yet.

"I wish I had a journal now," he said to the darkness. "I would write a good-bye letter to my family. Not that they would ever find it."

"You don't need paper to write a letter," said

Ruby. "You can write letters in your head."

"What do you mean?"

"You close your eyes and mouth and send your thoughts through the universe."

"But how can my family get a thought?"

"They'll feel it, even if they don't know it," said Ruby. "Don't you ever just get a feeling sometimes?"

*Yes.* Like sometimes at school, he could *feel* the Bull nearby, even though he couldn't see him. Same with Valencia.

"That's the universe sending you a letter," said Ruby.

He thought of Lola and how she always seemed to know what he was feeling. Maybe—somehow—she would feel that he was in trouble now.

"I think Lola gets lots of letters," he said.

"We all do," Ruby replied. "Some of us are just better at opening them."

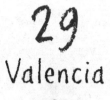

# 29
## Valencia

Forty-eight hours ago, I was just a regular girl observing wildlife. Now I'm walking with a psychic to the house of a boy I don't know so I can find out if he's missing or not. Life is funny, isn't it?

Virgil lives in a nice neighborhood, just like Kaori said. The houses are twice the size of the houses on my street. When I mention it to Kaori, she just says, "Yeah, yeah, his dad's a doctor." Then she waves it away like it's the least important thing to be thinking about right now. And maybe she's right. I was just making an observation.

To be honest, something about the big houses intimidates me, and I'm already nervous.

I'm not shy or anything, but I didn't really feel like knocking on the front door of a house belonging to someone I didn't know. But Kaori had explained once again that if Virgil's parents or Lola thought he was with Kaori when he was really off doing something else—something he shouldn't be doing—then he could get in big trouble.

"He probably isn't," Kaori had said as we made our way to the boy's neighborhood. "He's not exactly the type who goes off doing something he shouldn't be doing, just like he's not the type to miss an appointment. But you never know. People are an enigma."

So here I am, and Virgil's house is one block away. Kaori stops me, and she and Gen give me very serious looks, like I'm a spy going on a secret mission.

"Here's what you do," Kaori says. "Knock on the door and ask if Virgil's home."

"Thanks for spelling it out for me," I say.

When Gen giggles behind her hand, Kaori shoots her a look.

"I'm serious," says Kaori. "His Lola is very perceptive. I think she's one of us." She puts her hand on her chest to show me that "us" meant psychics. "If he's not home, just say thanks and say you'll stop back later. Then we'll know what's going on one way or another."

"And what if he *is* home?" I could already feel the heat of embarrassment. Maybe I wouldn't be so nervous if it was a girl's house, but the fact that it's a boy in a big fancy neighborhood makes my stomach flip around to the point of nausea. I don't exactly talk to boys on a regular basis. And I definitely don't go to their houses.

"Then tell him to come outside and meet us," says Kaori, glancing over my shoulder. "We'll wait right here."

Gen taps my arm and smiles up at me. "You don't have to worry that he'll freak out or anything," she says. "Virgil's really nice. And he's shy, like I said before. He even has a pet rat."

She pulls at the ends of her jump rope and shakes it loose. It splays across the hot cement and dangles near the toes of her sneakers.

"Really?" I say. This is an interesting development. Most people don't like rats, but they make good pets. Rats are really smart and curious. And they're always up for fun and adventure. It would be nice to have a pet rat. But I'd never ask my parents for one. I could just imagine the looks on their faces.

Now Kaori is tapping my shoulder so I'll know to look at her (she's really good at the how-tos), and at the same time giving Gen a little shove.

"It's not a rat," she says. "It's a guinea pig."

"Oh, I love guinea pigs!" I say. "I had one when I was really little, but it died. Her name was Lilliput."

I'd almost forgotten about Lilliput. She had very long hair and it was all different colors: light brown, dark brown, and black, mixed together. I can't remember where we got her because I was so little, but I remember feeding her hay and watching her drink out of the bottle in her cage. She died while I was at preschool. When I came home, my dad had already buried her in the backyard. I cried because I didn't get to say good-bye.

"Lilliput! That's a cute name," says Gen, as she positions her rope for jumping.

Lilliput is the name of an island from a book called *Gulliver's Travels*. In the book, the explorer, Lemuel Gulliver, travels to all these different lands after a shipwreck. The first place is Lilliput, an island where all the people are less than six inches tall. I liked the story, but I liked the name more:

Lilliput. It sounded just like a place where little tiny people would live.

I'm just about to tell all this to Gen and ask what Virgil's guinea pig is named when Kaori starts waving toward the house behind me.

"Hurry up, hurry up," she says. "We need to find out what's going on."

"All right, all right," I say. I turn and walk toward the house. I try to walk all nonchalant-like so they don't see how nervous I am.

There aren't any cars in the driveway. Maybe no one's home.

I walk up the stone pathway. It's not like the house is a mansion or anything, but it's big. Two stories tall, with a garage that fits three cars. There's even a knocker on the front door shaped like a horseshoe. I lift it up, knock three times, and wait. I play with the straps of my bag. After about five seconds, I decide no one's home. In one way it's a relief, but then again, it would be better if he *was* home, because that would mean that Kaori's friend is safe and sound.

Then the door opens. I know right away it's his Lola—which Kaori told me means "grandmother"—because she looks about a hundred years old. She's small, shorter than me, and really skinny. She doesn't smile. She's not exactly mean looking, but not exactly friendly, either. She glances at my hearing aids, but only for a second.

"Um," I say. "Is Virgil home?"

She lifts her chin like she didn't hear me correctly. Her hand is still on the doorknob.

"Virgil?" she says.

For a second I'm worried I didn't say his name correctly. Maybe his name isn't Virgil after all. Maybe I put the pieces of the puzzle together incorrectly.

"Yes?" I say. It comes out like a question.

"No, Virgil isn't home. He went out this morning. What is your name?"

My chest and neck feel hot.

"My name?" I reply stupidly.

"Yes," says Lola. "So I can tell him you came."

"Oh." I clear my throat. "My name is . . . um, Valencia."

"Um Valencia?" she says. I'm not sure if she's teasing me or being mean. It's hard to tell at first, but then her eyes soften and she smiles. "I was expecting you."

"You were?"

"Well, I was expecting *something*."

I expected her to say something normal, like "I'll tell him you stopped by," so I don't know how to respond.

"Your mother blessed you with a good name," she continues. "Valencia Cathedral is one of the most important cathedrals in the world. It's in Spain."

"Oh. I didn't know that."

"Maybe your mother does."

"I doubt it."

"Hmm." Lola looks like she's considering this. "You should tell her. She might like to know that she picked a good, strong name."

"I think she knows already," I say. "She's not the type to question her choices."

Lola laughs. Her whole face crinkles up when she does. She kind of reminds me of a cackling witch, but not in a bad way.

"I like your mother!" says Lola.

That makes me smile, although I'm not sure why, because I consider my mother to be the biggest pain in the world.

"Does Virgilio have your phone number?" Lola says. "I will tell him to type you a message when he gets home."

She motions her hands like she's tapping on a cell phone, and I realize she's talking about texting.

I could have just said yes, but instead I blurt out "No," which is the truth, and next thing you know, she's waving me inside so she can write it down. I look toward Kaori and Gen and shrug. They're too far away for me to see their faces. Gen is jump roping. She's pretty fast, too.

I don't realize how hot it was outside until I step into Virgil's house and feel the cool buzz of the air conditioning. Lola walks ahead of me, toward a big kitchen. I close the door and follow. She starts rummaging through a drawer. Her mouth is moving, but I can't tell what she's saying because she's looking at the drawer instead of me. It's funny how people talk to things like drawers instead of the person right across from them. I don't want to bend down and stare at her face, because that would just be weird. So instead I turn and look casually at this big bookshelf against the wall. I don't bother with the books though. Instead I stare right at a framed family picture. There are six people in the photo. Four of them are smiling—big, shiny, perfect smiles. Two of them aren't. One is Lola. She has a faint scowl on her face, like she's ready to get the picture taking over with. The other is a boy. He's not scowling, exactly. It looks like he's trying to make an effort to fake smile, but he just couldn't get up the energy. I know right away this is Virgil. And I know right away why Kaori's description sounded so familiar.

I know him.

I search my memory for his face, and it comes to me right away.

He's in the resource room every Thursday, just like me. We never talked or anything, but he seemed nice. Quiet.

When Lola taps me on the shoulder, I jump. Who knew I was so jittery?

She's holding a pen and scrap of paper and shaking it under my nose.

"Did you hear me?" she says. She's asking me to write my name and number on the paper.

"No, I'm sorry." I motion toward my hearing aids.

"There was a girl in my village who was deaf," Lola says after I give the paper back to her with my information. Virgil is going to be really confused when he gets it, but oh, well. What's done is done. "People talked around her like she wasn't there because they didn't think she was paying attention. They figure, no use hiding our secrets if she can't hear us. But she heard everything." Lola leaned forward and tapped the folded corner of her right eye. "She heard with her eyes."

I wonder what kind of secrets that girl knew.

"I hear with my eyes, too," I say.

"I know," Lola says. "I can tell." And she winks.

# 30
## Smaug

There were so many things you could do with a stick. That's why Chet liked sticks so much. You could poke and hit stuff. You could swing it around like a weapon. But most importantly—at least for today—you could root out snakes.

He hadn't seen a single snakeskin. He should have taken Davies with him and demanded that he point out exactly where he had found it. That would set him straight. Only Chet didn't want to share the spotlight when he captured the real snake. That glory would be his, and his alone.

He imagined just how it would go: him tying the knot on the pillowcase with the snake wriggling inside, then carrying the sack home like a triumphant bounty hunter. He would insist on keeping it as a pet, and once it was coiled inside its tank, he would call Davies right over and show him what he'd done with his bare hands. And that's exactly what he'd say, too.

"I caught it with my bare hands."

Chet wasn't so sure how his parents would feel about keeping a snake in the house. He could probably talk his mother into it. He seemed to be able to talk her into anything, especially if his father backed him up—but he didn't know how his dad felt about snakes. Chet liked to think his father wasn't afraid of anything, but he knew that everyone had their weaknesses. Even him. Chet would never tell anyone this in a million years, but despite being the bravest person he knew, he was afraid of dogs. Not little pipsqueak ones like Chihuahuas—he could feed one of those to his snake, no problem. No, it was the big ones that made him uneasy.

There were a few other things he was afraid of, too. Like the fact that he might not make the basketball team, no matter how hard he practiced. He'd already failed at Little League—never hit the ball, not even once—and Boyd Middle School didn't have football, so that would have to wait. Basketball was his best shot at becoming an athlete. *You might as well be nothing if you don't excel at something.* That was one of his dad's favorite expressions, and right now Chet was batting average at everything. Basketball could change that.

The snake could, too.

That was why he had a backup plan in case his parents wouldn't let him keep it.

He would ask his father to take a picture of

him holding it up, the way fishermen did with their big catches. Then he would text the picture to Davies with something clever, like "So you found a snakeskin, huh? Why don't you tell me the story again?"

Chet mentally crafted a series of clever texts as he walked through the woods with his stick and pillowcase. He scanned the ground as he went, looking for places snakes might be, like big thickets of brush where it was easy to hide.

"But you can't hide from me!" Chet bellowed, as if the snakes spoke English.

He wondered what he would name it after its capture. What was a good name for a snake? Killer? No, too juvenile. Cobra? Too obvious.

"Hmm," Chet said, jabbing a mound of leaves at the base of a tree. "Maybe Smaug."

Yes, Smaug. That sounded both threatening and snakelike. Besides, dragons and snakes were probably related.

When nothing slithered out of the leaves, Chet continued walking, yelling, "Smaug! Here, Smaug!" like he was calling a kitty. Each time he saw a pile of leaves and twigs, he jabbed and poked and called out for Smaug. And his heart didn't even pound. He was really made of some tough stuff.

And then . . .

*Swisssh.*

There was rustling in the leaves, similar to what he'd heard when he discovered that girl Valencia. He stopped and looked around. It was hard to tell where the sound was coming from. But he couldn't hear it anymore anyway.

He suddenly got the distinct feeling that he was being watched by someone. Or something.

"Hello?" he said. His voice sounded weak, so he tried to give it more gusto. "Is anyone there?"

No answer.

What if that deaf girl was hiding in the trees?

What if she was putting a hex on him?

He waited.

When nothing happened, he rolled his eyes and mumbled, "Whatever." He poked the leaves with his stick and heard something—this time, from the ground. He paused. Poked again.

He took a step closer so the toes of his sneakers brushed against the pile of leaves. He'd definitely heard something move in there. His body rushed with adrenaline. Goose bumps exploded across both arms, even though it was a million degrees outside.

He tightened his grip on the stick and swept away at the leaves.

He hadn't expected to find anything, really. Yes, he was on a snake hunt, but he'd been at it for hours, and now it'd just become something to do. He didn't realize that he no longer expected to find Smaug until he actually found him.

The snake immediately lifted its head. It was the width of a garden hose but not very long. At that moment Chet realized how little he actually knew about snakes. He knew how he would grab it—by the tail, of course, so he wouldn't have to put his hand near the snake's mouth. But he had no clue whether it was poisonous or not. Could snakes this small be venomous? How was he supposed to know? It probably would have been smart to do some research, but there was no time for that. He couldn't pull out his phone and Google it with Smaug's eyes on him. This was a once-in-a-lifetime opportunity. The snake was exposed, waiting for capture. The time was now.

Chet's heart thundered.

"Adrenaline," Chet mumbled. "Not fear. Adrenaline."

The snake wasn't doing anything. Just staring. Not hissing. It didn't sway back and forth like a sumo wrestler. It just rested there. Head raised. Almost like it was waiting to be picked up and petted. Almost like it was meant to be his pet.

Almost like fate.

Chet tossed the stick aside and flicked the pillowcase open with one melodramatic motion.

He took a big, deep breath and moved closer. The second he leaned in, the snake reared its head back and Chet wildly grabbed at its tail, which gave Smaug plenty of time and open air to swing around—one quick motion—and sink its fangs into the thick and ruddy skin of the Bull's right forearm.

It felt like the claws of a kitten digging into him. He knew what that felt like—his cousin had a vicious cat—but cats were one thing and snakes were quite another, so he immediately dropped Smaug and howled, certain he would die in less than five minutes.

His forearm turned pink right away. His skin burned. He imagined the poison traveling through his veins and attacking his heart. Who would find his body? That deaf girl? That retarded boy? And would they know how he died? If one of them found him, he'd at least like them to know that he'd died in a life-or-death fight with a vicious reptile.

He cradled his arm and stared at it. The pillowcase was crumpled in the leaves like a deflated balloon, and he suddenly realized that he had no idea where Smaug had gone. The snake had vanished. Chet walked about twenty feet from the scene of the attack, searching for it. Then he sat at the base of a sturdy pine tree and waited to die.

# 31
## Unpredictable Happenings

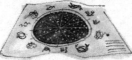

"Virgil wasn't home, which means he's in trouble. I know it," said Kaori. "We need to have the ceremony."

After they returned from Virgil's house, they'd collapsed on the floor of the Tanakas' living room to discuss their next plan of action. They'd also turned on the television, which had lured Gen's attention away. All for the better, as far as Kaori was concerned. Who needs the insight of a child where matters of life and death are at stake?

Just Renee frowned at the TV and said, "It's hard for me to make out sounds with the TV on in the background. Makes everything garbled." She wiggled her hands around her ears as if this was the universal sign for "garbled." "Do you mind if we lower it?"

Kaori glared at her sister. "Turn that thing down!"

Gen muted it, but didn't look away.

"Did you say something about a ceremony?" Renee asked Kaori.

Kaori's face turned serious. She straightened her back and folded her hands in her lap.

"The ceremony of lost things," Kaori said solemnly. "It's a ritual to help us find Virgil. But we can't do it here. We have to go into the woods. The ceremony only works if you're one with nature, and this certainly isn't nature." She gestured toward the television.

The clock on the wall—a hideously ugly and practical thing, in Kaori's opinion—said it was two nineteen. She wondered how long people had to be lost to be considered a missing person. It hadn't been that long, but a lot of bad things could happen in three hours and nineteen minutes.

Kaori anticipated Just Renee's next question: what's the ceremony of lost things? Truth be told, Kaori had no idea. She was sure there was a proper ceremony that could help gifted mediums find lost items or people; she just didn't know what it was. No matter. She would figure it out as she went along. The ancestors would guide her.

"There's no time to explain all the details," said Kaori. She stood quickly and snapped her fingers in her sister's direction. Gen turned her head, but not her eyes, from the TV.

Kaori sighed. Really, Gen was more trouble than she was worth sometimes. Kaori had explained that television was too practical, too traditional, too *everyday* for the Tanaka daughters, but the poor kid didn't seem to get it.

"Gen," said Kaori. "Get Mom's secret matches. We're going into the woods."

Mrs. Tanaka kept a box of matches in the second drawer under the microwave. She used them to light her secret cigarettes, the ones she thought she was hiding from her daughters. As if.

"You can't hide anything from me, Mother," Kaori had once said. "I inherited the second sight."

"Inherited from who?" her mother had asked. "No one on either side of the family has ever been remotely interested in such things."

Mrs. Tanaka had no appreciation for bloodlines or former lives—the kind that stretched back generations, the ones that no one knew about. When Kaori imagined her birth, she pictured herself emerging from a patch of lavender, dark haired and full of rage at the injustice of her past lives, of which there were two.

The first time she'd walked the earth, she'd been in ancient Egypt. She knew this because it came to her in a dream. She saw herself slipping between the pyramids in a long white robe. What other explanation was there, except that she had once walked through the pyramids in real life?

In her second life, she was a freedom fighter from Bangladesh. She knew this because she'd once seen a snippet of a documentary on television, and when they showed images of Bangladesh, they really looked familiar to her and she couldn't explain why. She probably could have learned more if her father hadn't switched the channel. She tried to explain that the documentary was necessary for her to explore past-life transgressions, but he said it was March Madness and past-life transgression didn't happen during college basketball season.

Just because her parents didn't know about her secret heritage and magical and mystical powers didn't make them not so. Besides, her parents had always been monstrously unimaginative. Take the smoking, for instance. Mrs. Tanaka smoked one or two cigarettes a week on the back patio, but she failed to consider that Kaori's bedroom window was usually downwind, which meant the smoke blew right by the spirit chamber.

Clueless.

Gen didn't make a move for the matches right away. Instead she took her precious time getting up so she could catch the end of her show. She didn't get a fire under her until Kaori snapped again.

"Life-saving missions don't wait for commercial breaks, you know!" she said. "Besides, we need to hurry before Mr. and Mrs. Tanaka get home."

Gen was still dragging her feet as Just Renee strode toward the door with her bag slung on her shoulder. Kaori snatched one of her mother's decorative candles out of the candlestick on the table, stuck it in her back pocket, and followed Just Renee outside.

Once the door opened, Gen picked up her pace. She grabbed her jump rope and slung it over her shoulder.

"Why do you bring that thing everywhere we go?" asked Kaori. "It's not as if we're going to jump rope through the trees."

"You never know when you might need to jump rope," said Gen.

Kaori rolled her eyes. "Really. You are a wonder."

She took the matches from her little sister, and the three of them stepped into the blazing hot sun.

"It's hot," Gen said. "We should cook an egg."

She'd heard somewhere that it was possible to cook an egg on a car or cement if it was hot enough outside, and she'd been needling Kaori about it ever since.

"We don't have time for science experiments," said Kaori. She locked the front door and shoved the house key deep into her pocket. Just Renee was already a few feet ahead, making her way toward the street.

"It only takes two seconds to crack an egg," Gen said.

"How can you think about eggs at a time like this?" Kaori asked. She and Gen followed Just Renee, who stopped at the Tanakas' mailbox to wait.

"I bet he's okay," said Gen. "He probably just forgot. What's the worst thing that could have happened?"

"You don't want me to answer that," Kaori said.

"Where are we going, exactly?" asked Just Renee.

"Yeah," said Gen. "Where are we going with the matches and candle, *exactly*?"

Kaori pointed straight ahead without breaking her stride, like a general leading her troops into battle.

"That way," she said.

As they crossed the street and entered the woods side by side, Gen tugged at Renee's sleeve.

"Do your hearing aids hurt?" she asked.

"Sometimes they itch or make a dent in my ear. Hurts a little," Renee said.

The trees brought much-needed shade from the heat. Kaori took note of their surroundings, thinking. She wasn't very familiar with the woods. Truth be told, they creeped her out. The woods were full of unpredictable happenings—snapping creatures, falling branches, stinging insects. She preferred the comforts of home, where she always knew what to expect. But what choice did she have? It's not like they were going to find Virgil hiding under one of the sofa cushions.

"Why do you still have to read lips if you have hearing aids?" asked Gen.

Twigs crunched under their feet.

"They don't make me hear everything clearly, the way you do. I have to fit the sounds with the shape the lips make, like a puzzle," Renee said, looking from Gen to the woods. "And then I have to fit the sounds and the shapes with the situation, because so many words look the same when you lip-read. Like 'mat' and 'mad' or 'pat' and 'pad.'"

"Were you born deaf?"

"No. I could hear a little. That's how I learned to talk. But then it went away, mostly."

"I wonder if mine will go away."

"Doubtful."

"Could you read lips from far away if you had binoculars or a telescope?"

Kaori couldn't take it anymore. How was she supposed to become one with the forest if Gen kept talking?

"Stop asking so many questions," Kaori snapped. She heard buzzing near her ear and swatted at it.

Gen blinked at her. "Why?"

"Because it's rude."

"Just Renee doesn't mind." Gen looked up at their new client and tapped her hand. "Do you?"

"*I* mind," Kaori said. "We need to stay focused, and your prattling isn't helping."

Kaori didn't want to admit it, but she liked having Gen as her second-in-command, which meant she was always first-in-command, which meant she needed to be in charge. But Just Renee seemed to be a natural take-charge person—she was leading the way, even though she had no idea what they were supposed to be looking for. Kaori would bet money she was a Leo.

"Let's stop here," Kaori said.

Gen stopped. Then Just Renee. They both looked at Kaori curiously.

"To properly conduct the ceremony, we need a special type of stone," said Kaori, with as much authority as she could.

"Like the five stones you told Virgil to get?" Gen asked.

"What five stones?" asked Just Renee, looking from little sister to big sister.

Kaori ignored the question. There was no time to explain minor details. "We only need one. It's called a snakeskin agate."

Just Renee tilted her head. "Did you say you need a snakeskin agate?"

"Yes. Snakeskin agate," Kaori repeated.

"What's that?" asked Gen.

"It's a stone. It could be as small as a pigeon egg." Kaori opened her empty hand as if the agate would magically appear there. "It's a rock with scales. That's why it's called a snakeskin."

Just Renee frowned. "We'll never find one of those in these woods."

"How do you know?" asked Kaori. "There's all kinds of rocks and things in here."

"Because snakeskin agates are usually found in dry riverbeds or along beaches—places where there's water." Just Renee looked around at the dry twigs and towering trees. "There definitely isn't any water around here."

Gen crossed her arms and raised her eyebrows at Kaori. "Now what?"

Kaori didn't know what to say. For all she knew, Just Renee was right. Kaori had never actually seen a snakeskin agate, after all, but she'd studied endless pages of gems online, and she knew which ones were used for what. The snakeskin agate helped you find lost things. And Virgil was lost; if not to himself, then to her. And as silly and ridiculous as Virgil was, she wanted to know he was alive and breathing.

"I suppose we don't necessarily need to find a snakeskin agate *precisely*," said Kaori. "Maybe just something like it. I mean, it's the gem you're supposed to use, but whatever. I guess we can just get a rock with scales. Something close enough. Maybe our energy will make up for the rest."

Gen looked up at Just Renee to gauge her reaction. "What do you think?" she asked.

Kaori frowned. She'd never heard Gen ask

anyone else for guidance before. Not even their parents.

Just Renee studied Gen's face, then looked at Kaori. A few seconds passed before she said, "If your sister says we need to find a rock with scales, I guess we need to find a rock with scales."

Kaori's shoulders relaxed. Something passed between the two older girls then, a mutual understanding that didn't need to be spoken—and Kaori, being a gifted person of second sight, had great appreciation for such things. She smiled at Just Renee, just a little, just a hint, and Just Renee smiled back.

That was when they heard the screaming.

# 32
## The Worst Things to Say

If Pah didn't get him first, Virgil figured one of three things would happen: he could suffocate, starve, or die of thirst. He didn't know which was worse.

Maybe all of them would happen. Maybe he wouldn't be able to breathe and his tummy would rumble until it made his heart stop and his throat would close up, dry as a bone, and it would all happen at the same time.

How much air was in an abandoned well, anyway?

Was there a limited supply?

Would it eventually run out?

Would Pah come back?

An army of tears surged up from his gut. He squeezed his eyes shut to stop them from gushing out, then looked up, up, up, trying to see if there were ways for air to get inside. But it was completely dark. If light couldn't get in, how would air ever make it?

"Doesn't matter much," said Virgil. "Since I'm gonna starve anyway."

He fed Gulliver a dandelion. He couldn't see him, but he felt the tug of Gulliver's teeth against the stem and heard the faint munching as he chewed it down.

"I'm sorry, Gulliver," said Virgil. "I got us into a big mess."

What happened next was inevitable.

It was bound to happen, even if Virgil didn't want it to.

Honestly? It would happen to anyone.

Virgil began to cry.

The tears pushed up from somewhere deep in his belly, shifted into his throat, and then dribbled out like water from a leaky faucet. He tried desperately to stop them. He hated crying. He hated how it made his face wet and his eyes puffy and his throat hurt, but there was no stopping it. The tears came harder and with ferocity, until the faucet wasn't just leaking, it was pouring, and Virgil had to catch his breath between sobs. Maybe he was being weak, or a baby, or a frightened turtle. So what, though? He was afraid. He was trapped in a pit without a friend in the world, and he was afraid.

He'd heard once that before you die, you see your life flash before your eyes. He wasn't exactly dying just yet, but a few flashes came anyway. He thought of Lola. He thought of her hands and how they felt like paper. He thought of all her stories, how she'd complimented his fingers and said he should be a pianist, and how she taught him about Pah and the Stone Boy and the Sun Queen. Too bad she'd never told him a story about how to escape a well. And now she never would.

He thought of his parents and brothers. The way they spoke in exclamation points and always teased him for being too shy, too quiet, and how they thought it was silly that he was afraid of the dark. He thought of how he used to imagine that he'd been floating in a river like Moses and his mother just happened to find him. Maybe she picked him up and said, "What's this! A baby with no parents! I'll take him home straightaway!" (Speaking in exclamation points, as usual.) And then he went home with her and everyone realized quickly that he didn't exactly fit in, but that was okay because they loved him anyway. And he loved them, too, of course, even if he didn't understand them. And now he never would.

And he thought of Valencia.

He wiped his snotty nose with the back of his hands and then swiped them on his pants. Usually he wouldn't do such a thing, but the rules didn't matter now. He was suffocating in a land of lost opportunities, where he should have talked to Valencia, told Lola that he loved her, tried to understand his parents and brothers, thanked Kaori for being such a good friend to him. And now it was too late for any of that.

Pah would come eventually, he was certain. And even if Pah didn't come—snatching Gulliver as an appetizer before going after the main course— there was still no hope.

Virgil took big, heaving breaths. He cried until the faucet ran dry. How would anyone find him? The Bull was his only hope for rescue, and there was a fat chance of that happening. The Bull had probably forgotten all about him already. Or maybe he was back in his devil's den, making a note in his log of evil deeds: *first day of summer, trapped Virgil Salinas in a well.*

Virgil's cheeks ached. His eyes burned. His nose throbbed.

Crying hurt. That's why he hated it so much.

"Crying is good for the soul," said Ruby softly. "It means something needs to be released. And if you don't release the something, it just weighs you down until you can hardly move."

"There's nothing else for me to do," Virgil said. His voice was hoarse from the weeping.

"You should try yelling again."

Virgil pressed the heels of his hands against his eyes. "What's the point? No one can hear me."

"Of all the questions you ever ask yourself in life, never ask, 'What's the point?' It's the worst question in the world," Ruby said.

"You sound like Lola."

"Good."

"I miss her." He said it quietly, embarrassed even in front of himself. But it needed to be said. When you say things aloud, you let them go. Lola had told him that once. But it didn't feel like it worked, because he still missed her.

"It's not like you're never going to see her again," Ruby said.

"How do you know? No one will ever find me. No one will ever save me. There's no chance."

"Bayani, of all the things you ever tell yourself in life, never say, 'There's no chance.'"

"Okay. It's too late, then."

Ruby sighed. The sound traveled like a curl of invisible smoke.

"That's even worse," she said.

Virgil slumped against the wall. He wanted to sleep through the starvation, but he couldn't. Not with Pah out there somewhere. Maybe Pah was just above his head now, watching. Waiting to swoop down. Circling, like a vulture. Virgil didn't dare look up to see. It was too dark anyway.

Just as Pah liked it.

Virgil held his breath.

Was that a feather against his cheek?

Was that a rustling?

He put his hands over his ears.

"Try yelling for help again," said Ruby.

"I don't want to. It might—"

"It might what?"

*Startle Pah from his invisible perch and send him down for us.*

"I told you, he only grows if you're afraid of him," said Ruby. "Ignore Pah. Just yell. Do it for me."

Virgil dropped his hands, slowly. All was quiet.

"You can't just give up," Ruby said.

"There's a time when a person has to give up. That's just the truth."

"Give me an example," said Ruby.

"I'm too tired to give examples."

"Don't avoid the question just because you don't want to think of an answer."

Virgil sighed. He thought for a moment. "Okay. Let's say you're running a race. It's a really, really long race, too. And you sign up because you think you can do it. You practice running for months, maybe even years. And then the big race comes and you're running and running. And suddenly your legs are really tired. And you're dehydrating. And you can hardly breathe. And the finish line is still way down the road and stuff. But you just can't make it. You start throwing up or something. If you keep going, you know you'll drop dead. So you stop. And you sit on the side of the road so you don't die. You have to give up, or else."

"That's a terrible example," said Ruby immediately.

Virgil's eyebrows bunched together. He glared into the darkness. "No it's not."

"Yes it is."

"What makes it a terrible example?"

"Because the person in your story didn't give up. Giving up would have been never starting the race at all."

Virgil sighed again.

"I want to sleep. Will you watch out for me?"

"I will . . . if you yell for help one last time."

"Promise?"

"I promise, Bayani. Make it a good one."

Virgil took a big, deep breath. He filled his chest with air, opened his mouth wide, and yelled and yelled until his voice gave out.

# 33
## Tanaka and Somerset

"Did you hear that?" asked Kaori. She had her hands up, palms out, as if to say "Everyone stop where you are."

Gen's eyes widened and her face paled. She took a step closer to her big sister. Then another. "I heard it."

"What? What? What happened?" said Just Renee, looking from one girl to the other.

"It sounded like . . ." Gen's eyes searched the

woods, but she didn't move a muscle.

"Someone calling for help," Kaori said.

Just Renee's eyebrows shot up. "You mean you heard someone screaming? Are you sure?"

"Yes," the sisters replied, in unison.

Kaori pointed westward. "It came from over there," she said.

Without saying another word, the three of them walked in that direction. A dozen images flipped through Kaori's mind. She imagined . . .

Virgil curled up at the foot of a weeping willow, holding a broken leg.

Virgil perched on the highest branch of the tallest tree. Trapped, like a cat. (Although she knew better— he would never climb a tree that high, if at all.)

Virgil lying next to a rock with a bump on his head.

She thought only of Virgil. She never imagined that after walking for two minutes they would come across something else altogether: a strange boy she didn't recognize sitting on the ground with his back against a pine tree and a white T-shirt wrapped around his beefy arm.

When he saw them, his face changed from frightened and whiny to frightened and irritated. His eyes went from Kaori to Gen, and then to Just Renee. When he saw her, he turned stoic and no longer seemed like the person who'd cried out.

"What are you doing here?" he demanded.

Clearly they knew each other. At least that's what Kaori's second sight told her at that moment.

"Did you scream for help?" Renee asked, sounding bored.

The boy huffed and turned away. He brought his arm closer to his chest. The three girls knew immediately that he had, even though he snorted out an unconvincing "No."

"What happened to your arm, then?" asked Gen, no longer ashen faced. She motioned toward the makeshift bandage, which Kaori now realized was a pillowcase, not a shirt.

"I was bitten by a snake, if you wanna know."
He sounded proud. "It was huge. Like a cobra. It
almost bit my arm off."

"Really?" said Gen, mesmerized.

"Yeah." His gaze swept all three of them. "I'm
probably gonna die if you don't get me to a hospital
or something. I'm sure it was poisonous."

Just Renee handed her bag to Gen and knelt next
to him. The leaves shifted under her knees. She held
out her hands and motioned for him to show her the
wound, like a mother dealing with a spoiled child.

"What're you gonna do?" The boy jerked his
injured arm away. "Hex me or something?"

Just Renee made a big show of rolling her eyes.
"I know a lot about snake bites, so just show me
your stupid arm."

"No way."

Just Renee dropped her hands and shrugged.
"Okay, then. But you should know that if you keep that

shirt or whatever wrapped around your arm like that, you'll probably have to get your arm cut off. You're not supposed to cover the wound that way."

The boy snorted again. "You're crazy. You're always supposed to wrap up an injury. Everyone knows that."

"When you wrap up a snakebite, it makes the skin warm and it traps the moisture. Moisture causes bacteria to grow. Then your arm gets infected. Then it spreads, and—" She made a chopping motion against her own arm. "That's why you're not supposed to wrap it up. Plus, I don't think it was poisonous anyway."

"How do you know?" Gen asked. She seemed disappointed, like it was much more interesting to meet someone near death from a bite rather than a stupid boy infecting his own arm.

Kaori observed everything with interest. Just Renee knew a lot about nature and animals. Maybe they should go into business together.

Kaori could tell the fortunes and provide spiritual guidance, and Just Renee could help her with spells or something. If Kaori needed a specific type of stone, Renee would know exactly where to find it. They could come up with a good name for their business. But not Kaori and Renee—that sounded lame. Something good, grown-up and businesslike. Their last names. Tanaka and . . .

Kaori tapped Renee on the shoulder as the boy reluctantly lifted up his wrapped arm.

Just Renee turned around to face her.

"What's your last name?" Kaori asked. "Just curious."

Just Renee paused, then said, "Somerset."

Tanaka and Somerset! That sounded perfect. Like a real business.

She could see the sign now, bright and blazing. She could almost feel the flashing lights burning her eyes. *TANAKA AND SOMERSET. TANAKA AND SOMERSET. TANAKA AND SOMERSET.*

When Just Renee tossed the pillowcase aside to expose the snakebite, Gen stepped forward and crouched next to them.

"That's it?" she said. "That's the big snake bite?"

Kaori looked at the injury. She'd expected to see something much more heinous, too, like an enormous bump oozing pus and mucus, but the boy's arm was red and that was it. They couldn't even see the fang marks.

"That's hardly anything!" said Gen.

"Of course not," the boy snapped. "When it bit me, I snatched it so hard with my other hand that it didn't have time to do any more damage. I pried its fangs out of my arm. Then I wrung its neck and tossed the body down that old well."

Just Renee glanced up at Kaori, like "Yeah, right."

"How do you know it's not poisonous?" Gen asked Just Renee. But Renee was looking at the boy's arm, not at Gen, so she didn't hear.

"Hey," the boy said, moving his arm to get

Renee's attention. She raised her eyes. Kaori suspected lasers would shoot out of them, if they could. "The stupid kid asked you something."

Gen yanked her jump rope off her shoulder like a whip, only it didn't look very threatening since it was hot pink and she'd put happy-face stickers on the handles. "What did you call me?"

The boy ignored her and repeated Gen's question to Renee. He held his arm against his chest like it was a precious jewel.

"Because this is barely a bite. You may as well have been stung by a wasp." Just Renee counted off on her fingers. "Your throat isn't closing up, you don't have a fever, you're not having a seizure, and you're sitting here talking to us like the usual dodo that you are. You probably got bitten by a water snake or a garter snake. Maybe a northern racer or something."

"Whatever, deafo." He scrambled up, off the ground.

"How'd you manage to get bitten by a snake,

anyway?" Kaori said, trying to make her tone as condescending as possible.

"I was on a snake hunt practically all day," he said. "That's what I do. I hunt snakes and kill them with my bare hands." He showed her his hands.

"Is that supposed to be impressive?" Kaori asked. "Sounds like you're mentally defective."

Just Renee stood, too. "You should go back to your cave and run warm water over that so-called injury. Then wash it with mild soap. You don't want it to get infected, or . . ." She made the chopping motion again. "And for the record, my name is Valencia, not deafo."

Gen and Kaori traded confused looks.

*"My name is Valencia."*

"I thought your name was Renee," said Gen, speaking for both of them. But Valencia had turned and was glaring at the snakebite victim as he walked away. So she didn't hear.

# 34
## Valencia

I must admit, it was a little disappointing to find out that the snake wasn't poisonous. Not that I'd want Chet's throat to swell up or anything—I would never wish something like that on anyone—but an arm infected with poison and a scary trip to the emergency room would have been nice. But then Chet would have a big, dramatic story to tell, so maybe it was for the best. I could picture it now: *"I went to the emergency room and almost died, man.*

*It was a close call for a while there. The doctors said I was lucky that I killed that cobra when I did. Good thing I had enough strength to demolish it and throw it down that well."*

Then again, he'll probably tell that story anyway.

After Chet walks off, I pick up the pillowcase like it's a dirty sock. I wasn't crazy about the idea of holding something that had touched Chet's sweat, but I'd already littered the woods with my mother's old bowls. The least I could do was throw this atrocious object away. I didn't want some squirrel family to find it. Or Sacred. The thought of Sacred cuddling up with something like Chet's pillowcase didn't set well with me.

When I glance back at Gen and Kaori, they seem confused, like they don't know who I am all of a sudden.

"We should go into business together," Kaori says.

"What?" I ask. I couldn't have heard that right.

"We should go into business together," Kaori says again. "I know about the spiritual world and you know about the natural world. It's the perfect partnership. That's probably why fate brought us together as friends."

*Friends.* Something about the way she says it makes me feel like I found something. I know it sounds corny, but in that moment, with that one word, I already feel like a different person. Is that possible?

"Or it could have just been a coincidence," I say.

"There are no coincidences," Gen and Kaori say, at the same time.

For some reason that makes us all laugh, and I don't care that I'm holding Chet's disgusting pillowcase anymore.

Once we stop laughing, Kaori's face turns serious.

"But first . . . ," she begins. "You have to tell us

the truth about something." She and Gen glance at each other. Gen is still holding my bag, so I reach out for it. "Is your name really Renee?"

I stand up straight, as straight as I can, and put my bag on my shoulder. "No," I reply. "My name is Valencia. Valencia Somerset." Just like a battle cry.

# 35
## V. S.

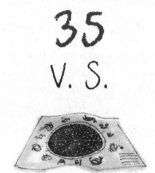

Kaori was certain she had never heard the name Valencia Somerset in her entire life, but something felt very familiar about it. Like having déjà vu. Something in her brain clicked and said, *This is important, pay attention.* But she couldn't figure it out. She pressed her lips together tight and tried to force an answer into her vision, but nothing came. It felt so close. Like she could reach out and touch the answer, if only she knew where it was.

*Valencia Somerset.*

Renee had straightened her back when she announced her real name, like she was proud of it. Kaori was fond of her own name as well. It was critical to feel empowered by your name—Kaori believed that with all her heart.

"We should keep looking for the stone," she said. "Virgil's been missing for hours. Let's get back to work."

Gen's face lit up. "I know! Maybe we don't need the snakeskin stone now because we have an actual snake*bite*!" She pointed at the pillowcase that Valencia still had pinched between her thumb and index finger. "Well, not an actual snakebite, but snakebite *juice*, anyway. That's gotta count for something!" She looked at her sister expectantly.

*Hmm,* Kaori thought. Maybe Gen had a point. Surely saliva from a snake's actual *mouth* had to count for more than a rock, right? It made logical sense.

"What do you think?" Kaori asked Valencia.

Never in all her days—not even in her past lives—
had she ever asked another person for guidance or
advice, but if they were going to be business part-
ners, now was a good time to start. Kaori knew the
importance of collaboration in running a business.

Valencia nodded. "Makes sense to me."

But they were interrupted again when Valencia's
phone buzzed. The vibration was so loud that Kaori
thought it was her own phone at first.

"It's my mom," Valencia said when she saw the
message on the phone. She announced it like she'd
just been given six hours of homework. "She wants
to know where I am. Ugh." She rolled her eyes. The
pillowcase dangled at her side. Kaori was reminded
of pictures she'd seen in history class, when people
waved white flags to surrender.

"Do you have to go home?" asked Gen, whiny
and weighty with disappointment.

"Technically," said Valencia.

Kaori was about to say that the ceremony

wouldn't take long and maybe Valencia could sneak in an extra fifteen minutes before she had to go, but then the bells of the Buddhist monastery sounded and Kaori had to look at her own phone, too. It was her mother. It was like parents were all on the same wavelength or something.

"It's Mrs. Tanaka," Kaori told her sister.

But the text wasn't asking where she was or when she was coming home.

> Have you seen Virgil
> Salinas, by any chance?

Kaori's heart dropped. The fact that her mother was asking meant that someone had asked her, which meant it was one of Virgil's parents or brothers or Lola, which meant that they didn't know where he was, either. Which meant this was a true-blue emergency of epic proportions.

Kaori texted back.

No. He was supposed to come over at 11 but he never showed up.

She started to type more details—that they were looking for him now, that they were going to have a ceremony, and so on—but if she did that, Mrs. Tanaka might tell her to come home with Gen right away, so she deleted the few words she'd written and waited for her mother's reply.

"She asked if I knew where Virgil was," Kaori said, sounding just as sullen as she felt.

Something was wrong.

Something was very wrong indeed.

"That means his parents are looking for him." She turned toward Gen. "So he didn't get held up at home like we thought. And he hasn't been home since Renee—uh, Valencia—went over there."

Gen frowned. The three of them were quiet for

a moment, until Gen's face suddenly lit up, just as it had before.

"Hey, maybe he went off with V. S.!" she said. "Maybe they ran away together, like in the movies."

"That's impossible," said Kaori. "Yesterday he could barely say her initials without choking."

Valencia's phone buzzed again.

"It's not impossible," said Gen as Valencia texted on her phone. "Maybe he sent her a message last night or this morning and they're off right now, eating popcorn at the movies, just him and V. S."

"You watch too much television," Kaori said. "There's no way he 'ran off' with V. S. That doesn't make any—"

She stopped midsentence.

"What's the matter?" Gen asked.

Now she understood the déjà vu.

The reason Valencia's name seemed so familiar and important.

*Valencia Somerset.*

Kaori tapped Valencia on the arm. When she looked up, Kaori asked, "What's your sign?"

Valencia put her phone away and raised an eyebrow. "Why?"

"Just tell me. Are you a Scorpio?"

Valencia hesitated. "Yes. How did you know?"

"And do you go to the resource room on Thursdays at your school?"

Valencia tilted her head suspiciously. "Yes. Why?"

Gen jumped up and down three times. "Ohmygod, Kaori! *She's* V. S.! *She's* V. S.!"

"Yes," Kaori said, all serious business. "She's V. S."

"What's going on?" Valencia asked, puzzled. "I can't understand what you're saying."

Kaori moved quickly to stand next to her sister, then clamped a hand over her mouth. "We can't tell you."

"Why not?"

"Just because."

"That's not an answer," said Valencia. "Obviously it has something to do with me, so I deserve to know." She shifted her eyes to Gen. "So what is it?"

"We can't tell you because it would interrupt fate," Kaori said. She still had her hand over Gen's mouth.

Valencia looked like she wanted to laugh.

"I'm serious," Kaori said. "Fate has directly influenced this entire day so far. It's all clear now."

"Come on," said Valencia. "Tell me."

"It will all make sense once we find Virgil."

Kaori could feel Gen's excitement bubbling under her palm, ready to explode.

Valencia put her hands on her hips. "I won't help you find him unless you tell me."

"What if his life is in danger? You'd put his life in more danger just because I won't tell you something?"

Valencia's face fell. Her arms dropped to her sides. "I guess you're right." She jabbed a finger in

Kaori's direction. "But you have to promise to tell me once we find him."

Kaori let go of Gen so she could put her hand on her heart. "I promise it will make sense when we find him."

"*If* we find him," Gen added.

"When," said Kaori. *"When."*

# 36
## Maybe

Virgil was tired. Plain and simple. He was still afraid, hungry and thirsty, but mostly he was tired. He'd been right all along. There was no point in yelling for help because no one could hear him. No one would come. All the hours of being terrified had drained him. He was too exhausted to even worry about Pah.

*"Bayani, of all the questions you ever ask yourself in life, never ask, 'What's the point?' It's the worst question in the world."*

Ruby. What did she know?

Since this was the end of Virgil and Gulliver, he hugged his backpack close to him and decided to take a nap. But he didn't want to fall asleep thinking about all the ways he'd failed in life, so he decided to imagine what he would do differently if he was ever rescued.

One: he would stand up to his mother and say, "I wish you wouldn't call me Turtle anymore." And then she would say okay, and he could just be Virgil or Virgilio or whatever. Or the family could come up with a new nickname for him, like Bayani.

Two: next time the Bull called him a retard, he'd speak up. "Call me that again, and you'll regret it," he'd say. There wouldn't be any shake in his voice. He wouldn't just say it, he'd mean it. Maybe he'd even fight him. Or maybe he wouldn't need to because the Bull would know he meant business—no questions asked.

Third (and most important): he would talk to

Valencia. Even if just "Hello." One word. That's all it took to strike up a friendship, right? One word could make all the difference.

He said it now, in his tired and weary voice. "Hello. Hello. Hello."

It sounded muffled and anguished. That's how everything was down here, though.

"I'm tired," Virgil said to no one. "I'm going to sleep. I don't care if Pah eats me." He tilted his head back. "Do you hear that, Pah? You can eat me. Just leave Gulliver alone. I'm going to sleep."

His Lola had once said the world looks different through newly opened eyes. Maybe if he went to sleep, he would be home again when he woke up and he could do those three things. Maybe he'd be tucked into the warmth of his bed, listening to Gulliver's cage rattle as the guinea pig drank his water.

Maybe.

# 37
## Valencia

You shouldn't light candles in the middle of the woods, especially if it hasn't rained in days, but we're standing in a small clearing and Kaori insists it's vital to the ceremony. The good news is, she also says it's vital that I make a circle in the dirt with my foot and drop the snake-juiced pillowcase in the middle of it, and I am more than happy to get rid of it.

The candle isn't lit yet, but Gen has the matches

 276

ready. She seems disturbingly eager to use them.

"First we say the chant, and then we light the candle," Kaori says.

"What's the chant?" I ask.

My phone vibrates in my pocket again, but I ignore it. What's the big deal if I don't come home right this minute? Besides, I'm doing something really important—trying to help someone find a friend. Not that my mother would understand.

"It goes like this," says Kaori. She closes her eyes. "Keeper of lost things, guide us to what we seek. We send this heartfelt request to the universe of granted wishes." She says it slowly and deliberately.

I wait for more.

"Is that it?" asks Gen.

"Yes. Then we light the candle and wait."

"Wait for what?" I ask.

"Wait for the answer to come to us."

I must admit, I think this whole thing is kinda weird and silly, and I'm not sure I believe in fate and all that. But I would like to be Kaori's business partner. I'm sure we can work something out. I decide to talk to her about it later, when we're not in the middle of a ritualistic ceremony.

"Ready?" asks Kaori. "We have to say it all at the same time."

We stand very still.

Kaori repeats the sentences. We say them together at the same time.

Gen strikes the match.

When I told Kaori not to light a candle in the middle of the woods, I didn't expect that we would actually start a fire, but that's exactly what happens. Gen strikes the match too hard and it dives out of her fingers and into some dry leaves outside the circle. They flame up in no time. They aren't big forest-fire flames. They remind me of the burners on our gas stove at home. It's not panic-worthy, but that doesn't stop Gen from screaming at the top of her lungs. Kaori and I stomp out the fire, and I decide right away that I like the idea of being friends with someone who isn't afraid to step on flames.

The fire is out, but Gen keeps screaming anyway. I look up and realize that she's not screaming about the fire anymore. She's pointing over my shoulder. So I turn.

Sacred!

He bounds toward us. A canine on a mission.

He immediately comes up to me and barks once, like he wants to make sure everything is okay. That's the thing about dogs. They know when you're in trouble.

The air smells like burned leaves.

"This is Sacred," I say. "He's harmless. I take care of him sometimes. He lives in the woods."

Kaori wraps her arms around her little sister, but Gen's freak-out seems to have disappeared just as quickly as it started. She shakes Kaori off and scratches Sacred's ears.

Kaori looks at the remnants of the fire. "Now

what are we gonna do?" she says. "The ceremony is ruined, I think."

I start to answer, but my phone goes off again, and I figure I should check it or else it will just vibrate and vibrate until it drives me out of my mind.

When I look at the screen, I see about five million missed texts from my mom, but there are also two messages from a number I don't recognize. The first one says:

> Hello, Valencia of Spain!

And I know right away that it's from Virgil's Lola. The second one says:

> Have you seen my Virgilio?

It's funny how the mind works. I hadn't realized there were clues this whole time, leading us to

Virgil. But as soon as I see that text, something or someone—Saint Rene, maybe?—unplugs a clog in my brain. Just like that, a flood of realizations swamps me, one after another.

The path we took to Virgil's house from the Tanakas' led straight through the woods. And Virgil had been on his way to Kaori's house for his appointment. He'd probably take the same path, wouldn't he?

*"I was on a snake hunt practically all day,"* Chet had said. *"That's what I do."*

So Chet was in the woods at the same time as Virgil. Chet, who never let me pass him at school without some idiotic gesture. Chet, who made fun of David Kistler every day in science class. Chet, who was a bully.

Then I remember the little collection of stones I'd found that morning. Something Gen had said earlier echoes in my head. *"Like the five stones you told Virgil to get?"*

And I'd thrown them down the well, one by one.

*"I wrung its neck and tossed the body down that old well."*

Odd how the well cover was open. It was *never* open.

That's why I had closed it—so the squirrels wouldn't tumble inside.

My breath catches in my throat.

I turn to Kaori slowly, with Lola's message in front of me.

Sacred nudges my hand.

"I know where he is," I say.

# 38
## Light

*"The world looks different through newly opened eyes, Virgilio. It's the trick of time. What you believe today, you may not believe tomorrow. Things change when you're not looking. And then you open your eyes, and you see—"*

Light.

Was that light?

Virgil had drifted off. A few hours ago he wouldn't have thought it was possible to sleep when your life was in grave danger, but he'd actually fallen asleep, cradling Gulliver close to him. All the crying, fear, and loneliness had wrapped a big, heavy blanket around him and told him to rest, so he had. But now the darkness on the other side of his eyelids shifted and there was light, like when his father flicked on the switch to wake him up for school. One minute, darkness. Next minute, light.

But there couldn't be light, could there?

And there couldn't be noise, right?

People calling his name?

It sounded like someone was calling his name. Or maybe a few people.

Did he hear a dog bark? That didn't make sense either.

He didn't want to open his eyes because he didn't want to find out it was all a dream, or a trick, or that he was dead and this was the light that everyone talked about. If he opened his eyes, it wouldn't be real. He wouldn't hear Kaori and Gen calling out,

"Virgil! Virgil!" and then a third voice—a girl's—that sounded like a voice he knew, but it couldn't be. That was the sign that it was all a trick. It wouldn't make sense for Valencia to be up there with Kaori and Gen. They didn't even know each other.

This was proof that he was dead, not being rescued.

But they called again.

"I think I see him," Gen said. "But it's dark. I can't tell."

He opened his eyes.

He saw light.

He saw the silhouette of three heads, all looking down at him. One of them was certainly Kaori. He could tell by her hair.

He blinked. And blinked again.

"Hello?" he said. His voice was quiet and hoarse. "Hello?"

*"Louder, Bayani. Louder!"*

"Hello!" he called. "Hello!"

"He's in there! He's in there!" It was Gen. Her voice filled the well with a different kind of light.

"Virgil, it's Kaori! We're going to rescue you!"

"Oh," Virgil said. "Good."

He wanted to say more—much, much more—but that's all he managed.

He stood up. His legs tingled with numbness. He checked on Gulliver, who regarded him with shaking whiskers.

"We're being rescued," he said.

Gulliver chirped. Virgil shifted his backpack from the front to the back.

"Valencia and Gen are here with me!" Kaori called down.

Something about the way she said it made him think that she knew who Valencia was. But how did they know each other? How did Kaori find her? And had Kaori said anything?

Suddenly Virgil was overcome with embarrassment. But that didn't matter now. First he needed to be rescued. Then he could be embarrassed.

"How come you can't just climb up the ladder?" yelled Kaori. "How did you get stuck down there?"

"The bottom of the ladder is missing," called Virgil. "I can't reach it from here."

The three heads looked at each other and murmured a discussion.

"We're trying to figure out the best way to rescue you," Gen informed him. The discussion continued for several more seconds. He couldn't hear anything until Gen said, "Wait a minute! What about this?"

Virgil couldn't see what "this" was, but he didn't much care, as long as he was getting out.

"That's a great idea!" It was Valencia. "I'll do it."

He swallowed. Valencia was there with Kaori and Gen. *Valencia.*

Could it have been the stones, each of a different size? Or was it just a coincidence?

*"There are no coincidences."*

Someone was coming down the ladder, holding

something. A rope, maybe. How had they found a rope?

It was Valencia—coming down faster than he'd done hours before, but slowly enough to watch her step.

Be careful, he wanted to say. Please be careful.

His heart pounded.

He cleared his throat.

When she reached the bottom rung, she dropped one end of the rope into the well and said, "Take this and I'll tie the other end to the ladder. Then you can pull yourself up, like a mountain climber."

He couldn't see her face because of the darkness, which meant she couldn't see him. He was glad for that.

He reached for the rope. A jump rope.

"That's my jump rope, Virgil! I grabbed it before we left the house!" Gen called down proudly. "Isn't that lucky?"

*Yes,* Virgil thought. *Very lucky.*

# 39
## Valencia

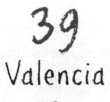

It's hard not to believe in fate when you watch a boy climb out of a well using a jump rope.

The first thing he does when he emerges is look inside his backpack, and that's when I see the guinea pig. I take a step closer so I can get a good look. Sacred is next to me, but I shoo him back just in case Virgil doesn't want him around his guinea pig. Not that Sacred would eat him or anything. At least I don't think he would.

Virgil is as still as marble. It's like he's been frozen in place.

Kaori and Gen are both asking a million questions at the same time, and even though I can't make out all the words, I know they're asking if he's okay, if he's hurt, if he needs anything, that kind of stuff. I see that he's alive and breathing, even if he isn't really speaking.

"I used to have a guinea pig," I say.

Kaori and Gen stop talking. We all look at Virgil. They're waiting for a response, and I'm studying his expression so I can understand him when he talks. But he doesn't say anything. He has a weird look on his face, like I just shined a flashlight in his eyes or something. He shifts from foot to foot and turns to Kaori. In times like this I usually assume the person is ignoring me, but Virgil doesn't seem like the kind of person who does things like that.

Maybe he's in shock after all those hours underground. I can't imagine being trapped like that, especially since there's not much to explore in a well. But all things considered, he's not too bad off. His eyes are red and puffy—I bet he cried—and his clothes are dirty, but other than that, he looks like the same boy from the resource room.

"I'll buy you a new jump rope," he says to Gen.

I can barely hear him.

Kaori's eyes move from Virgil to me and back to Virgil again. It reminds me of how my teachers look when they're waiting for someone to figure out one of their word problems.

"Who cares about that stupid old jump rope?" says Gen. "Tell us everything. How did you get in there? What happened? What did you do all that time? How long were you in there? What did Gulliver do? Were you scared? Did you think you were going to die? How much longer would you have lasted, you think?"

"Honestly, Gen, do you ever stop asking questions?" Kaori says.

"You just asked one," Gen replies.

Virgil glances at me. There's a red splotch on his neck, and it inches its way to his face like someone's painting him from the bottom up.

"Gulliver got trapped down there," he says. I can barely understand him because he speaks so quietly and he's looking at Kaori again. "I had to go down and get him."

I turn to Kaori. "Gulliver?" I say, to make sure I heard him right.

"That's the name of his guinea pig," Kaori explains.

"My guinea pig was named Lilliput," I say, to Virgil.

There's a flash of recognition on his face—he knows the story, too, I can tell. But then he presses his lips tight like someone's zipped his mouth.

"Virgil," says Kaori, looking at me so I'm sure to hear her. "Do you know Valencia? Valencia Somerset? You know her, right?"

The way she says it is weird. Like she's giving Virgil some kind of clue. But what?

He nods.

We all stand there.

"Lilliput is an island in *Gulliver's Travels*," I say, since no one else is speaking. "Isn't that a coincidence?" Kaori and Gen both open their mouths, but before they can say it, I put up my hand. "I know, I know. There are no coincidences."

My phone vibrates again. It's my mom.

She isn't happy.

> I'M WORRIED. WHERE R U? COME HOME NOW

All caps. That's not good.

I sigh. "I really have to go. My mom is freaking out."

Kaori shoves Virgil in the shoulder, hard. Sacred lumbers around, just in case it's the start of something, then pauses at Virgil's side and lazily wags his tail.

Kaori's gesture says, This girl just pulled you out of a well, aren't you going to at least say thank you?

But I don't mind that he's being quiet. Some people are shy, that's all. It doesn't mean he doesn't have manners. I know what it's like to have people waiting on you to say the right thing, even if you don't know what the right thing is. That's how I feel when people forget the how-tos.

But Kaori is insistent. She raises her eyebrows and makes a motion with her hand. Go on, go on.

Virgil looks at his feet. I think his mouth is moving, but I can't tell what he's saying, if anything. But there's no time to figure it out. If I don't get home soon, my mom will have a one hundred percent total breakdown.

I promise to text Kaori about Tanaka and Somerset, then I just wave and say, "See you later."

It feels anticlimactic after everything, but sometimes things don't end the way you expect them to.

# 40
## There's No Hope for You, Virgil Salinas

It was almost too much for Kaori to handle. The universe—the big, mysterious, fickle universe— had plotted everything out to the littlest detail (with her influence, of that she had no doubt), and Virgil barely mustered two words.

"What was that?" she said. "I mean—what was that? She's V. S.! And you didn't even talk to her!"

Virgil's face flushed. Full-on red now. He put his

hand on Sacred's head and ran his fingers along his fur.

"What do you mean?" he said.

Valencia was now out of sight, but Kaori waved in her general direction, rolled her eyes, and heaved an enormous sigh all at once, to show the level of her displeasure.

"You barely spoke! This was your chance, Virgil. School's over. She just rescued you from a well—"

"Hey, I'm the one who had the rope," said Gen.

"And you just stood there! I thought this was the girl of your dreams or something. Fated to be friends."

Virgil's face now resembled a ripened strawberry.

"What do you mean?" he said unconvincingly. "I just met her."

Kaori crossed her arms. So did Gen.

"Virgil Salinas, I know when people are lying to me, and you are officially the worst liar in the universe, which is really sad because the universe *itself* is trying to intervene on your behalf."

Virgil looked at Sacred.

Sacred looked at Virgil.

"The universe isn't doing anything, Kaori. If it was, then it wouldn't . . ."

He paused.

"Wouldn't what?" Kaori said.

"Nothing."

"If it's not the universe, then how do you explain everything that happened today?" She counted on her fingers. "The fact that V. S. came to see me on the exact same day you disappeared. The fact that she somehow figured out where you were. The fact that Gen had a jump rope."

"Yeah," Gen offered in support. "What about all that stuff?"

"And lest we not forget," Kaori continued, raising her finger in the air for emphasis, "the fact that she had a guinea pig with the same name as yours."

"It wasn't the same name. Her guinea pig was named Lilliput."

"Might as well have been the same thing!"

Kaori would have kept going, but a text from her mother said it was time to come home for dinner.

Virgil looked at the dog. "Kaori, all that stuff is just . . ."

"Don't say it," Kaori said.

"It was all just . . ."

"Don't say it," Gen said.

". . . coincidence."

Kaori hung her head. "If that's what you believe, there's no hope for you, Virgil Salinas." She turned to her sister. "Come on, Gen. Mrs. Tanaka made chicken cutlets."

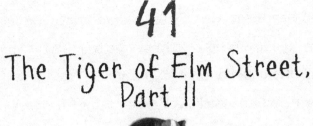

# 41
# The Tiger of Elm Street, Part II

All he had to say was two words. Just two words. "Thank you." Valencia Somerset had pulled him out of a well, and he didn't even thank her. He hadn't said a single word. Not even hello. How hard was it to open your mouth and talk? Why did he have to be so . . . Virgil-like?

"Hello, Valencia," he mumbled to himself as he made his way down Elm Street with Sacred, who walked right alongside him as if they were connected by an invisible leash. "Thank you. You practically saved my life. I owe you one."

His body ached. Hunger pains seared through his empty stomach. His head throbbed like it had its own heartbeat. He was scuffed and dirty. He could have died. But he could have at least said "Thank you." He could have at least said "Hello."

Sacred's paws click-clacked against the sidewalk. Virgil was acutely aware, as always, that he was fast approaching the Bullens's house, but he was too exhausted to care. Being face-to-face with death made Chet seem so . . . ordinary. Boring, even.

Virgil wasn't sure if fate was testing him, or if it was just your usual Saturday evening luck, but the Bull was outside as they approached. He was sitting in the middle of the driveway with the basketball in his lap, staring up at the hoop like it was a million miles away.

"Hey, retardo," said Chet when he saw him.

Then he saw Sacred and scooted back a little.

Virgil didn't put his head down like he normally did. He didn't shuffle past and hold his breath until he was safely out of harm's way. He was too tired, too fed up, too everything. Today was not the day to mess with Virgil Salinas.

Well, not anymore.

Virgil made direct eye contact with Chet, and before he even knew what he was doing, he stopped.

Sacred stopped, too.

The Bull pulled up his knees and wrapped his arms around the ball. His eyes darted from Sacred to Virgil.

"What're you looking at, retardo?"

Was that a tremor in his voice?

Virgil's arms hung at his sides. Sacred nudged his hand.

"Call me that again, and you'll regret it," Virgil said.

The Bull's uncertain smile faded. He cleared his throat.

"Whatever," he said.

*"It doesn't take many words to turn your life around, Bayani."*

Lola was waiting outside when Virgil came up the walk. He was barely within hearing distance when she started.

*"Ay, naku!* I've been calling and typing to your phone! Where have you been? And what is that animal doing with you? And why didn't you answer—"

Now that he was closer, Lola could see the rumpled clothes, the unkempt hair, the sheen of sweat and fatigue, his puffy eyes, the dirt and rust on his hands from the ladder. And he must have had a certain look on his face, because after she assessed his clothes and hair, she fixed on his expression.

"Virgilio," she said quietly. "What's happened to you today?"

"I got eaten, like the Stone Boy. But my friends chiseled me out," he said. His voice was tired and weary. He walked past Lola and opened the front door. She followed him inside without any more questions. So did Sacred.

His parents and brothers were in the living room, but they didn't seem overly concerned with Virgil. They were watching television—something funny, of course—and filling the room with their laughter. His parents were on the couch with their backs to him, and his twin brothers were in recliners on either side.

His mother turned at the sound of the door. When she saw Sacred, she stood up and waved madly.

"Get that dog out of here, Turtle! He'll mess up the rug!" she said.

The others turned then, too.

"A dog will be good for the house," Lola said. "Keep away the robbers."

She exchanged a knowing look with Virgil.

His father said, "Sit down and watch television with us," and he turned back to the TV, apparently unmoved by the presence of a large, strange dog.

Julius and Joselito half stood from their seats to get a look at Sacred.

"What kind of dog is that?" Julius asked.

"Where did you get him?" asked Joselito.

"I don't know. He followed me home," Virgil said.

At that moment, Virgil realized how bright his house was. Even its smells were comforting; he hadn't noticed that before. And the cool air felt plush on his skin.

His mother had made her way around the couch and was shooing Sacred. The dog took two steps toward the door, then two steps back to Virgil, confused by Mrs. Salinas's frantic movements.

"Turtle! He's dirty! And he stinks!"

Lola put her hand on Sacred's head. The dog stood still.

"He just needs a bath," said Lola. "Virgil will give him a bath. Won't you, Virgilio?"

She lifted her chin and gave him a look. It was a look that said, "I understand."

Understand what, though?

*"You are not the same Virgilio. That's what she understands. Open your eyes, Bayani."*

Virgil blinked. He put his hand on Sacred's head, right next to Lola's.

"I wish you wouldn't call me Turtle," he said to his mother. "You can call me Virgil. Or Virgilio. Or Bayani. But don't call me Turtle."

She stopped her panicked movements and stared at him. He'd never seen this look before. He didn't recognize it. Anger? Sadness? Shock?

*"She's seeing you for the first time, Bayani. That's all."*

She kissed her index finger and pressed it to his forehead. "Okay, Virgilio," she said.

# 42
## Messages

There are seventy-three new text messages on my phone, all between me and Kaori. We're figuring out our business plan. Tanaka and Somerset. I almost suggested that it should be alphabetical order—Somerset and Tanaka—but since it was her idea and she's more of the expert, I figured her name should come first.

There are seventy-three new text messages on my phone.

Yesterday I only had twelve, and most of those were from my mom.

It's nearing midnight now. The room has been dark for hours except for the light of my phone. I'm yawning, and Kaori and I have finally decided to save the rest of our conversation for tomorrow. But we have a solid base plan. Our next move will be finding clients.

Before we sign off, I have one question.

> what were you and gen
> talking about before we went
> to the well? You said it would
> make sense once we found v

Kaori didn't say anything for a long time—or at least what felt like a long time. Finally she texted back.

> When it's time for the
> universe to speak, it will.

307

If I'm going into business with her, I guess I should learn how to say things like that. Or at least try to understand what they mean.

I think I kind of have an idea, though.

It's not that different from how I talk to Saint Rene.

I don't know if Saint Rene is listening.

I don't know if Saint Rene is even able to listen.

For all I know, Saint Rene no longer exists and I'm just talking to nothing.

But Saint Rene *might* be somewhere, listening and nodding and helping me along.

Who knows?

I lay the phone on my chest and shake my Crystal Caverns globe. I watch the bats flutter and fall. I got my wish to be an explorer. A well is kind of like a cave, right?

I close my eyes and rewind the day. I've never helped a snakebite victim, saved a boy from a well, and met a psychic all in one day, so there's a lot to rewind. Life is funny sometimes.

Yesterday I had twelve texts on my phone.

Today I have seventy-three.

I think about everything, even Gen's jump rope.
I picture it dangling there, from the last rung. How
many years would it take before her jump rope rots
and disappears? Maybe—maybe—it would rescue
some other kid, a hundred years from now. I imagine
what that kid would look like. It could be a boy again,
or a girl. And their friend dares them to go into the
well, and they do. And they fall. And they think they're
stuck and they'll never be able to escape, until they
see the rope. And they'll think it's fate. They'll wonder
how that rope got there, and they'll never know.

The rope will shine—a bright pink coil in a
dark, dark place.

I like that thought.

It's like we've left something behind.

I don't know for sure, but I don't think I'll
have the nightmare tonight. Don't ask me how

I know. Sometimes you just know.

I think about Lilliput. And Gulliver, too. I wonder if my mom will let me get another guinea pig, if I ask her.

I think of Sacred. What was he doing at this moment?

And I think of Virgil, too. The way the redness crept into his face. The way he wasn't able to talk. I think of how he looked in that family photo, like he only went because his parents made him, which was probably true.

Thinking of Virgil makes me think of his Lola. "Valencia of Spain!" she'd said. I remind myself to learn more about the Valencia Cathedral. She said it was an important place, and she seemed like she knew what she was talking about. I wonder what makes it important.

I wonder what cathedrals look like, and if I'll ever go to one.

I yawn again.

My eyes are still closed. I feel myself falling down, down, down into sleep. I'm almost there when something jolts me awake. I jump. My eyes open. The room seems lit by a flashlight—only it's not a flashlight. It's my phone. And it's vibrating.

Kaori must have forgotten to say something.

I pick it up. My eyes burn because the screen is so bright.

It's thirty-three minutes after midnight.

It's Lola's number, but I know right away it isn't Lola.

Suddenly I'm wide awake.

I stare at the single word, and for some reason, I don't know why . . . I get a weird feeling in my belly, like a hundred butterflies have taken flight.

It says:

hello

# Acknowledgments

The universe wants to thank the following people.

First: Gina Oliva, PhD, retired Gallaudet professor, Deaf advocate, author of *Alone in the Mainstream: A Deaf Woman Remembers Public School*, and coauthor of *Turning the Tide: Making Life Better for Deaf and Hard of Hearing Schoolchildren.* Thank you for your patience, kindness, and friendship. I'm further indebted to the invaluable insight of Janet Weinstock, also of Gallaudet; American Sign Language instructor Karen Kennedy; the Deaf-Hearing Communication Centre of Swarthmore; and the wonderful Beth Benedict, past president of the American Society for Deaf Children.

I would also like to recognize Nancy Kotkin; John Murphy; Davy DeGreff; Ayesha Hamid; Rebecca Friedman; Kelly Farnsworth; Laurie Calkhoven; Shonda and Aiden Manuel; Rosaland Jordan; the Rosemont College MFA program; the Highlights Foundation; the super-incredible team at HarperCollins; my super-incredible agent, Sara Crowe; all my family in the US, Philippines, and beyond; the wondrous artist and illustrator, Isabel Roxas; and all the teachers and librarians who have supported my kidlit journey.

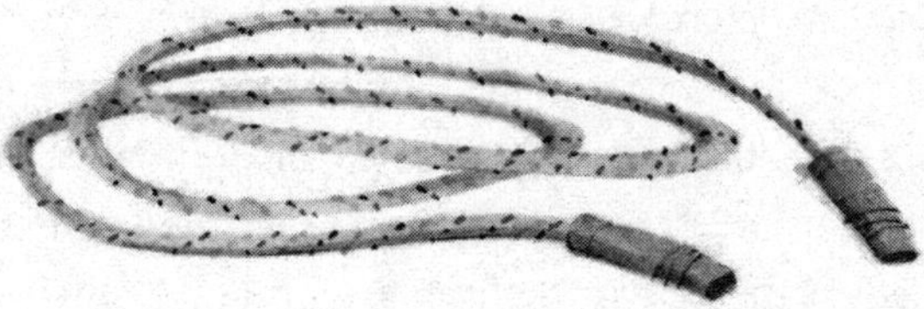